LITERALLY GONE

A PEPPER BROOKS COZY MYSTERY, BOOK 3

ERYN SCOTT

KRISTOPHERSON PRESS

Copyright © 2018 by Eryn Scott

Published by Kristopherson Press

All rights reserved.

erynscott.com

erynwrites@gmail.com

Facebook: @erynscottauthor

Sign up for my newsletter to hear about new releases and sales!

No part of this book may be reproduced in any form or by any electronic or mechanical means, including information storage and retrieval systems, without written permission from the author, except for the use of brief quotations in a book review.

Cover by Paper and Sage Designs

 Created with Vellum

For you, Mom.
Always present, a constant friend, your influence beyond all other.

(Dedication with help from Jane Austen)

1

It is a truth universally acknowledged, that a bibliophile in possession of her own bookstore, must be in want of… well, nothing really. What more could one ask for?

I sighed contentedly as I looked around the dusty, sunlit shelves of Brooks' Books—*my* store. The heady, almond and vanilla scents of the worn books mingled pleasantly with the crisp, freshly printed smell of the new volumes, creating the most satisfying medley I could imagine. The shop, steadily busy from summer tourists, was even more crowded today.

Today marked the start of Pine Crest's annual Austen-Fest—a week-long fair of food, books, and theater devoted to Lady Jane. I'd volunteered the bookstore as headquarters for ticket sales and was pleasantly surprised to see how many people bought something from the store as they purchased their tickets for the event.

Customers mingled around a table of Austen-inspired gifts, running their fingers across the covers of ornate notebooks, pricking their fingertips with the points of decorative quills, and giggling at the Jane Austen action figures I'd special ordered for the event.

My boyfriend, Alex, stood behind the register, leaning against the counter with a book folded in half in one hand. The man was harder on his books than anyone I'd ever met. He bent them, never carried a proper bookmark, and by the time he was done with them, they looked like they'd been through war. As a customer approached with purchases in hand, he set the book face down, spine up on the counter. I had to look away from the strained and cracked spine.

Hamburger, my Boston terrier and official shop dog, wound her way through the aisles—and sometimes right through the customers' legs. Her tongue lolled happily as she gazed up at the shoppers, hoping for a pat on the head or a scratch behind the ear. I knelt and called her to me. She trotted over.

"How's the shop, girl?" I plucked a small dust bunny off her nose, giggling. "I think we might need to up our biweekly dusting to every other day, huh?" Hammy snorted in response and then ran over to her bed behind the register. She pounced on her chewy toy as if she'd forgotten it was there until now.

I followed her to the counter, arriving just as Alex handed the woman her bag of books.

"Have a good day," I told the customer, then I looked to Alex. "Thanks for helping out on your day off," I said, planting a kiss on his cheek.

The fact that he liked books almost as much as he loved his job as a local police officer meant I never had to beg him to spend time here. I let a hand trail around his middle as I scooted around to access the computer.

"Anytime." He caught me as I moved past him and pulled me into a longer kiss.

We'd known each other the better part of a year, but had only been dating officially for a few months, a touch longer than I'd owned the bookstore. Honestly, I couldn't believe how much time I'd wasted knowing him and *not* being able to kiss him.

When he pulled away, I eyed his poor, abused paperback still splayed out on the counter. It was *Pride and Prejudice*.

"First time?" I asked, gesturing to the book.

"Yeah. It was on Mom's list." He shrugged. "I also figured I should brush up on my Austen for the festival."

He tried to hide it, but I could see the slight tightening in his face as he mentioned his mother. She had been a cop as well, but had been shot in the line of duty over a year ago. The woman had loved reading classics and he was making his way through as many as he could in an attempt to stay connected with her. It was actually one of the ways Alex and I had grown closer. We'd had a bit of a rocky start to our friendship, but bonded over both having lost a parent—my father passed away from a heart attack nearly two years ago.

The small bell rang out from above the door as it swung open. Nate Newton, the local coffee shop owner, strode inside. The lanky man blinked his beady eyes as he surveyed the shop. As he stared a few customers down, I swear it looked like he was thinking of the best way to cut them up. Creepy as Nate came across, I was getting to know him better lately, and was finding there was a pretty nice guy behind all of his unsettling gazes.

"Good afternoon," Nate said. Even though he'd grown up here in Washington, he had a slight British accent which still had me scratching my head. He bent in a slight bow, but was so tall that even bowing he still seemed to tower over everyone. When he straightened again, his eyes met mine. "Pepper, do you have any more tickets? I ran out earlier this morning."

"Sure." I grabbed the envelope next to the computer

and fished out a handful of tickets. While the fair itself was free, people could purchase admittance to daily, outdoor productions of Austen-inspired plays which would take place on a grassy knoll in the park next to the festival. "How many do you think you'll need?"

He pursed his lips forward, highlighting his few, scraggly mustache hairs. "Twenty should be fine."

I counted them into a pile, then handed them over. As Nate thanked me, the bell over the door rang out again. This time a hush blanketed the store, save for a few gasps and the odd whisper. I glanced up to see who had elicited such a response.

My eyes narrowed as they locked onto, none other than, Thomas King. Around me, whispers rose.

"Is that really him?"

"He's so hot."

"I can't believe he's here."

"He grew up here. Didn't you know that?"

The whisperers grew louder, bolder, and their words wound around me until they felt suffocating.

Thomas King *had* grown up here. He was my older sister Maggie's age and had been picked up for a supporting role in a popular, angsty teen drama on television the day of high school graduation. The guy had skipped town right after the ceremony. He and Mags had actually been dating during the time and he hadn't even broken up with her before leaving. Barely containing a scowl, I thought about how he'd never given her so much as a goodbye.

He placed his sunglasses atop his mop of messy, dark hair, winked at a woman to his right, and then strode over to us as if he were walking down the red carpet at an awards show. Hamburger growled. I picked her up.

"Pepper Brooks? Is that you?" His voice was just as smooth as ever.

"Tommy, I can't believe it," I said sweetly, loving the way his jaw tightened at the sound of the name he'd gone by growing up, the one he'd dropped as soon as he'd left.

He cleared his throat. "It's Thomas," he corrected. "Thomas *is* my—" He stopped himself, closing his eyes and taking a deep breath through his nose. "Never mind." He flashed his big, bright smile at a few more customers and winked at a handful of others. His gaze settled on Nate and recognition flashed over his features. "Naked Newt?" Tommy's voice rang out, loud enough to bounce off every surface in the bookstore.

Nate flinched and my fingers curled into Hamburger's fur. No one really used that nickname anymore, especially not to his face. But Nate, Tommy, and my sister had all been in the same graduating class, and it appeared that Tommy and Nate's antagonistic dynamic hadn't changed.

"What are you doing here, Tommy?" I asked, unable to mask the irritation dripping off each word.

He cocked an eyebrow. "I'm here to star in *Pride and Prejudice*. You know, for old times' sake—to help out the town. Uncle Phil said he mentioned it."

I exhaled. *Ugh*. Phil King was the president of the Pine Crest Chamber of Commerce, and therefore, thought he ruled the town. At our last meeting, he *had* said, "Wouldn't it be great if we got Thomas here for AustenFest this year?" I'd figured he was simply talking about a visit. Closing my eyes, I shook my head.

"Tommy, it's—parts have already been cast. This isn't…" I felt Alex's hand land softly on my shoulder for support. I glanced at him and then back at Tommy. "Have you talked to Bonnie about any of this?"

"Who?"

"She's the director."

He shrugged. "I heard you were in charge."

"Of ticket sales only."

Ignoring me, he changed the subject. "Hey, how's your sister?"

Bristling, I pushed back my shoulders. "Happily married to a great guy. Has two beautiful kids. So... she's *great*. The best." I could feel heat curling up my neck.

"Kids?" Tommy asked, his nose wrinkling. "That's too bad. She used to have such a great body." He shook his head.

"She still does," I said defensively. Hammy barked, as if agreeing with me. "She's got a fantastic body—it's—" I stopped when I felt Alex's hand tighten on my shoulder.

He was right to cut me off. That had gotten weird. Fast. I shot a quick thank you glance at Alex.

When I looked back, Nate, who seemed like he was trying to stab Tommy with his eyes, said, "Margret's skin is as creamy and taut as—"

I held up a hand to stop him. The creep factor of what he'd already said was super high and I really didn't want to find out where he was going with that. I'd always suspected Nate was in love with Maggie. Usually it weirded me out. Today I welcomed his support. I just didn't really need the details.

As if Nate wasn't currently eye-murdering him and Alex wasn't standing right behind me, Tommy added, "Then it must run in the family." His eyes swept up and down my body, making me shiver in disgust.

"Excuse me?" Alex asked, his hand tensing where it held me.

Before my boyfriend could punch this guy in the face, I

stepped forward. Hammy growled again, obviously upset at being closer to the man. "Tommy, this isn't going to work. They already have all of the actors lined up, and honestly, there's not enough time for you to learn the lines."

"Psh." Tommy shrugged. "I'm going to be playing Mr. Darcy. *Pride and Prejudice* is always the last play of the week, so I have *days* to memorize my part. Plus, what does Darcy have, like seven lines? All I have to do is look broodingly handsome and we both know I can do that."

Before I could voice even one of the *many* corrections I wanted to make to the blasphemy he'd just spouted, Tommy spun around to face the crowded bookshop.

"What do you say? Do you guys think I can do Mr. Darcy justice?" He smirked and ran a hand through his hair.

I almost threw up in my mouth.

The customers cheered and a line formed behind the counter as they rushed toward the Festival Tickets Sold Here! sign.

Clenching my teeth tight for a second so I wouldn't scream, I pulled in a deep breath through my nose. Handing Hammy over to Alex, I forced my mouth into a smile and asked the first woman in line, "How many would you like?"

"That depends. Is Thomas King really going to play Mr. Darcy?" she asked, pausing to shoot Tommy a flirtatious glance as she reached for her wallet.

Swallowing a groan, my thoughts returned to a conversation I'd had with Bonnie, the director, yesterday. She'd been worried about how few tickets we'd sold so far and had asked if I had any ideas on how to get the word out.

"It's my first year directing and I want this to be a hit." She'd wrung her hands nervously as she'd paced around the bookshop.

This being my first year selling tickets, I'd been unable to help her. Now, looking at the giant line forming in front of me, it appeared there was something we *could* do. I also knew, from experience, that Tommy and the Kings usually got their way around Pine Crest. If he wanted this, it was only a matter of time before he or his uncle convinced the director to follow along.

I sighed and Tommy flashed me a smug grin.

"I can't say for sure. It's a change he'll have to run by the director." I shrugged, unsure of what else to say.

The woman hesitated for a moment and then said, "What the heck. I'll take three." She pulled out her money.

Tommy winked, waved, and turned to leave. "See you around, Peppy," he said, using the terrible nickname he'd given me growing up. "I'll expect my schedule and a script by tonight at the latest." He strode out the door before I had a chance to respond.

AN HOUR LATER, I was out of tickets and patience. I swiped at my sweaty forehead and looked around at the now mostly empty store. Tommy seemed to have sucked out most of the energy—and customers—when he'd left. And while Nate had slunk out soon after Tommy, Alex stayed around to help with the remaining patrons. He wrapped an arm around my shoulder.

"So that guy was the worst," he said, once we had the place to ourselves.

"Tell me about it."

I spent the next few minutes filling Alex in on Tommy's breakthrough part on television. I loved how Alex shrugged, unimpressed, when I mentioned the name of Tommy's show.

"Frank's going to be *way* too excited about this," Alex rolled his eyes.

His partner on the force, Frank Fitz, was a large, jovial man in his late thirties. He had a laugh that shook his whole body and an obsession with all things Hollywood.

Cringing, I nodded. "Yeah, when the town found out Tommy had gotten the part all those years ago, Frank started a local fan club for the guy."

"You grew up together?" Alex asked.

I nodded. "He and Maggie dated for a few months, even. They were both theater nerds. Well, until he got cast as the lead in some of the school plays and his ego inflated faster than an emergency life-raft. Then he left and seemed to forget they were ever together." Letting out a frustrated groan, I said, "I can't believe he thinks he can play Darcy."

"Sounds more like a Wickham to me," Alex said.

I'm pretty sure my eyes turned into hearts as I smiled up at him. "I've never found you more attractive than I do in this moment," I said.

Alex waggled his eyebrows up and down, tucking his paperback into his jeans pocket. "Oh yeah? I've got more where that came from." He winked and leaned forward, planting a kiss on my cheek. "But it's gonna have to wait. I've got to head to the station." He glanced at his watch.

"I thought today was your day off."

"It was, but Dad decided to take off for a couple of weeks, so I'm gonna help pick up the slack since they'll be down a man."

I narrowed my eyes. Alex's father, Detective Valdez was serious, surly, and super focused. I couldn't picture him taking a day off, let alone more than a week.

As if anticipating my question, Alex answered, "It's Mom's birthday on the sixteenth. He had a really hard time last year, so I told him to take off, go clear his head. He has a buddy down in California he used to hike with. They're going to do some backpacking."

Swallowing the lump in my throat, I tried to meet Alex's downturned gaze. "And what about you?" I asked, placing my hand over his.

Meeting my eyes, he smiled then snaked his arms around me. "I've got you to keep me company."

I smiled as he kissed my neck.

Alex sighed then stepped away. "Okay, I really have to go."

"See you later," I said as he walked toward the front door.

I picked up the phone to call Bonnie. A pit sat in my stomach as I thought about telling her what had happened.

"Thomas King back in Pine Crest," I muttered to myself, shaking my head as I dialed the number.

2

"Hello?" Bonnie's twenty-year-old assistant, Sarah, answered the phone.

"Hey, Sarah. It's Pepper. So I have good news and bad news. The good news is that I sold a bunch of tickets today…"

"That's great!" Sarah said in her usual, perky way. She was a perpetual cheerleader, that one.

"Erm… yeah…"

"Oh, right. You said bad news, too." Her excitement dissipated quickly.

I explained Tommy's impromptu appearance in my shop this morning and his announcement.

"I'm sorry," I said. "I made sure everyone I sold tickets to knew it wasn't for sure. I did sell out, though. I don't know, Sarah. At first I was looking forward to Bonnie telling him no and sending him packing, but he might be really good for festival business."

Sarah was quiet on the other end. My gut twisted, worried I'd really messed up.

"Um… okay. Yeah. This'll be fine. It'll be great. I—" She took an audible breath. "It's just a bit tricky, is all."

"I know, it's so last minute."

"Well, that and the fact that it was Will who was supposed to play Darcy."

I grimaced. Will was Bonnie's husband. "Oh no."

"Yeah." Though I couldn't see her, I had a feeling Sarah and I were making similar faces.

"I'm so sorry. I hadn't heard that." I shook my head. "I would never have put her in this position if I'd known. Usually I pay more attention to who's playing which parts. But this year, I've been so busy with the ticket sales, I haven't had a chance to look."

"It's okay, Pepper. I'll… talk with her. You've done what you can. She and I will take it from here."

I thanked Sarah and hung up, but despite her assurance that they had everything under control, I felt worse and worse as they day went on. AustenFest's first performance, *Mansfield Park*, started at two o'clock, so only a few more customers trickled through the store after my phone call. I was happy to have the break, taking care of some ordering for the shop.

Just as the sun was beginning to dip closer to the mountains out my front window, my phone beeped with a text message. It was from my best friend and roommate, Liv.

> I want to check out this nerd festival you've been talking about. Wanna meet me for dinner? Or are you too busy sniffing books?

I chuckled and shook my head. Liv was my opposite— the pantsuits and briefcases to my leggings and books—but we were still inseparable four years after getting randomly placed together in a freshman dorm. Even though we lived together we had barely seen each other all summer, both busy with new jobs.

Happy as I was to hear from her, Liv's mention of the festival reminded me of my conversation with Sarah. I still felt awful about putting Bonnie in such a hard place. Maybe I could stop by and talk with Bonnie, tell her in person how sorry I was and see if there was anything I could do. That might make me feel less guilty, at least.

I texted back,

> You're in luck! I have a break in my sniffing schedule.

Grabbing my purse from under the counter, I glanced over at Hammy, sleeping in the dusty sunlight by the front window. "Wanna go see Liv, girl?"

Ears perking up, Hammy jumped and raced around me in circles as I attempted to hook her leash onto her collar. I chuckled and turned the sign from open to closed, then locked the door behind us. I hated that I had to close the shop when I needed to leave, but without an employee to watch over the place while I was gone, I was forced to do so. Everyone seemed to be at the festival, however, so I didn't think I'd be missing out on too many sales.

Even in the evening the summer sun shone, and everything seemed to be either a bright green or a light blue. My bare arms soaked up the heat and Vitamin D happily as Hamburger and I walked the few blocks to the park that housed the festival.

As we turned the corner, I spotted Liv walking from the opposite direction, coming from the town's university. Her blond hair was swiped up into a high ponytail and she had on a smart gray business suit.

I waved, my mouth pulling into a big smile. Not only was it good to see my friend, but I could already smell the festival foods. Liv greeted Hammy.

"Aren't you dying in that?" I asked, plucking the lapel of her suit as she stood.

She slipped out of her jacket. "Completely."

The girl had grown up in Seattle, not too far from here, so she shared my Washingtonian tendency to melt if the mercury hit anything higher than seventy-five.

Draping her jacket over one arm, she led the way toward the tents. "My office is air-conditioned and I've been spending so much time in it, I think I forgot the sun existed."

Liv had recently started a job as the assistant director of accounts at Northern Washington University and had been putting in crazy hours—hence the fact we had to schedule time to hang out.

"Aww, but you wanted to see me so badly you made an exception?" I placed a hand over my heart.

Liv's eyes swiveled between me and the festival. "Er... yeah... *you*, not the fried food and desserts. Sure." I could feel her gaze pulling away, focused on the tents and old-timey pennants whipping in the wind.

I laughed and bumped my shoulder into her as we walked down the first row of booths. The smell of delicious foods swirled around us. Hammy stuck her nose in the air and sniffed as we walked across the grass, trampled down already by so much foot traffic.

As we walked, I filled Liv in on the mistake I'd made and how I was going to try to make amends.

"It doesn't sound like there's much else you could've done, Peps," Liv said, eyeing a meat-pie booth. She patted me on the back. "You gotta stop being so hard on yourself."

"Thanks." I nodded, hoping it would help me convince myself to do just that. Hammy pulled on her leash, obviously excited. We picked up the pace a little.

The place was packed. *Mansfield Park* appeared to have just finished, and the audience members joined the already busy festival. I held my hand up to shield my eyes from the sun, currently flashing evening light on the grassy expanse of Pine Crest Park, so I could read the signs set up at each booth. Vendors were dressed to the nines in their finest Regency attire.

I licked my lips as I passed by the Meryton Meals tent, remembering past years' festivals with baked apples, single-serve trifle cups, and puddings. Liv and I grabbed some meat pies from another vendor, eating them as we walked and chatted about our days. Just as we ate our last bites, we came upon Nate's latte stand, a temporary outreach from his brick-and-mortar café, Bittersweet.

While not incredibly "Regency" sounding, the specials he'd created for the event made my mouth water.

"Lavender Cardamom Latte and Turmeric Chai Latte," Liv read the sign out loud.

"Good evening, ladies," Nate said from behind a foldable table. "And hello there, Hamburger. What's your poison?" he asked us.

"Hey, Nate," Liv greeted him, ignoring the eeriness of his question. She was used to the way he spoke as if he were playing Mad Libs with a serial killer's personal journal. "One of each of the special *poisons*, please."

"Coming right up." He bowed slightly.

"I was only kidding about the poison." Liv laughed, her face pulling into a nervous smile. "You know that right?"

Nate cackled way too loud. "Olivia, I think we both

know the answer to that. Don't we now?" He spun on his heel and walked to the espresso machine.

Liv blinked, eyes cutting to me then back to him with nervous speed. "Uh, do we? We *should*—but I feel like maybe I need to specify it was a joke—" Liv said, getting louder until she realized he wasn't listening to her. She finished with a quiet, "No poison, please." Her head dropped forward and she pinched the bridge of her nose.

I patted her back. "I'll never understand why you think you can be sarcastic with him."

Liv groaned. "I can't seem to control it."

"Look, I'm sure he doesn't actually have poison." Hamburger growled from where she stood at our feet. At first I thought she might be trying to tell me something about Nate and his ability to get his hands on poison, but then I glanced to my right and saw the last person I wanted to see. "Ugh. Not again."

Tommy. *Twice in one day?* How had I become so unlucky? His little sister, Ana, followed behind him. I hated how festivalgoers and vendors alike gawked or snapped pictures of the "celebrity" with their cell phones.

My fingers dug into Liv's arm. "Run," I whispered, eyes wide.

But before Liv or I could act, I heard, "Are you following me, Peppy?"

Taking a deep breath, I ignored Tommy's question and said, "Hey, Ana," as I waved half-heartedly at the willowy girl with long, dark hair standing next to him.

Ana King was a soon-to-be piano star and valedictorian of my class. We'd never been very close in high school, but Ana had been invited to everything because of her sweet demeanor, so she had been at every sleepover, road trip, and party throughout our years in school. She'd been gone, off at Juilliard for the past four years and had just returned to town a few months ago.

She waved back, sending me a sweet smile. "Hey, Pepper. Good to see you." I had only heard she was back, but hadn't yet bumped into her. "Is this your dog?" she asked, pointing down.

I nodded. "Yeah. This is Hamburger, and this is my roommate, Liv."

Ana waved at Liv and then cocked her head as she focused on Hammy. "Hamburger?" she asked.

"My niece named her," I said with a shrug.

"Okay, that's pretty adorable," Ana said, laughing.

I joined in, a little surprised. Ana had never said much in high school, preferring to stand back and people watch, so having a conversation with her was beyond what I was used to.

Obviously uninterested in anything that didn't have to do with him, Tommy's eyes settled on Liv who had glanced in his direction. He gave her a wink and said, "Recognize me, sweetie?"

Liv pressed her lips into a thin line and cocked her head to the side. "Hey... yeah. Aren't you the guy from those erectile dysfunction commercials?"

Tommy's face tightened slightly in discomfort. Snorting quietly, I pretended Hammy's leash needed fixing. I had the *best* best friend.

When I looked back up, Tommy was rolling his eyes. "I'm sure you know *exactly* where I'm from. And it's *not* that." He turned toward me. "I still don't have my script, Pepper."

I thought about what Liv had said, about not being so hard on myself. This wasn't my problem. It was Tommy's. He'd created it and he needed to fix it.

Pushing back my shoulders, I said, "That's because you have to go talk to the director about that." I stepped closer to him. "She's married to the guy currently cast as Darcy, too, so I'd watch what you say around her."

Tommy appeared nonplussed. "I'm sure they'll both understand. You can explain it to them when you go get the pages. Heck, think of what it'll do for this guy's reputation to be *my* understudy."

Blinking, I said, "I think you may be overestimating that honor, Tommy."

"He is." Will, Bonnie's husband, appeared behind Tommy. He was in his late twenties and had that tall, dark, and handsome look. Perfect for playing Darcy, I thought, as opposed to Tommy's brand of tall, dark, and high-maintenance.

The pink left Ana's porcelain features as she stepped slightly behind her brother.

Tommy huffed, dipping his chin in a tight greeting. "Will. It's been a while."

I'd forgotten Will was only about five years older than Tommy, so they would know each other, had probably even done a few plays together before Tommy left for Hollywood.

"See you're back in town," Tommy added, not even having the decency to *act* sorry as he faced the man he planned to displace.

Will pushed back his shoulders and took a step forward. While he and Tommy were close to the same height, Will had a good fifty pounds of what looked like mostly muscle on the twenty-five-year-old. Their similar appearances and angry faces made them look like the same character years apart.

"I am." Will watched Tommy. "So are you."

"Oh, only temporarily," Tommy said. "How about you? Is your move back temporary?"

Instead of answering the question, Will leaned in close and said, "You think you can come here and take over something I've worked for?"

Tommy, clouded by confidence or stupidity—I couldn't tell which—stood his ground. Even though he didn't say anything, it seemed like enough of an answer for Will, who stepped even closer. Hammy growled, as if anticipating what was about to happen.

But before things could escalate any further, Nate called out our order from his booth, making me jump. "Two specials!" He caught sight of the almost-kerfuffle next to his tent and eyed the men.

Relief flooded through me as I watched the two wannabe Fitzwilliams separate slightly.

"Newt! We meet again. A barista, huh?" Tommy strode forward, his voice curving into a Southern Californian accent I *know* he didn't have growing up. He looked cool as a cucumber, but I knew him talking to Nate was more about getting away from Will and less about wanting to catch up with his old schoolmate. I watched Will storm away in an angry huff.

Tommy glanced back only for a second—probably to confirm his possible attacker was gone—then focused on Nate again. "I didn't know you were working at Bittersweet, man."

The tension broken, Liv and I walked toward Nate, Hammy trotting behind. I reached out for my drink at the same time Liv went for hers.

Nate ignored Tommy as he held out our drinks. His fingers lingered on our cups for a second before he let us pull them away. "Your *non*-poisoned drinks, my dears."

Liv shook her head. "See? I have no idea if that means they *are* or *are not* poisoned," she whispered.

Placing his spindly fingers gently onto the table, Nate blinked and finally acknowledged that Tommy had been talking to him. "I own Bittersweet, actually," he said slowly, eyes piercing the man.

"Own? Never thought you had it in you, Newt." There was an indefinable quality to Tommy's voice that made me certain he didn't mean it as a compliment.

By the way Nate's fingers were turning white from pressure, I'd say he'd picked up on it, too.

"So, owner…" Tommy stepped up directly across from Nate. "Can you make me a doppio con panna?" He watched Nate, cocking an eyebrow when the man didn't respond. "No? An affogato then?"

Nate stayed silent.

Tommy chuckled. "Okay, how about a regular ol' quad-shot vanilla latte? Think you can handle that?"

The disdain written so plainly in Nate's eyes sent a chill through me. I stepped forward. "He can totally make one of those. Can't you, Nate?" I willed him to meet my gaze instead of continuing his fierce stare into Tommy's.

After a second, Nate turned to face me, his features immediately relaxing.

"Nate's a genius behind the espresso machine," I added, giving him a wink of encouragement.

Tommy snorted. "We'll see. I have been living in L.A., though, so don't feel bad if Pine Crest doesn't *quite* live up." He tossed a crisp five-dollar bill toward Nate and then walked off to check his reflection in a mirror in the clothing booth next door where Ana had wandered.

Liv and I smiled at Nate, waiting for a moment to make sure he seemed okay. When he started Tommy's drink, we let out a collective breath and then walked away. Hamburger tugged at her leash, as if wanting to go after Tommy, but finally followed.

"Okay, I might have gotten scared about Nate poisoning our drinks just a minute ago," Liv whispered, taking a sip of the lavender cardamom latte. "But from the way Nate's glaring at him, I'd say this Tommy fella is the one we should really be worried about him killing."

After a gulp of the turmeric chai, I nodded. "If Will doesn't beat him to it."

3

We walked around the festival for a little longer until Liv had to get back to finish up some work.

"Here, let me take Hammy with me," Liv said. "She'll be my excuse not to stay too late tonight."

I nodded, handing over the leash. "Okay. And if that works, I think you should start bringing her to work more often. You've been putting in crazy hours."

She sighed. "I know. It's just learning this new position. Everything will calm down eventually."

I pulled in a deep breath and nodded, watching her warily. Upon closer inspection, I noticed her usually tidy ponytail was slightly messy and her always perfectly pressed suit was a little rumpled. My energetic, perfectionist, tough-business-lady best friend seemed to be in danger of burning herself out.

As if she could read my mind and wanted to avoid a conversation about her workload, Liv waved and headed off before I had a chance to say anything more.

I *was* going to head back to the bookstore, but most of the town was here and I'd already finished all of my ordering earlier today when it was slow. Now would be a perfect time to go talk to Bonnie, apologize, and make sure there wasn't anything I could do to help. Instantly feeling better at the thought, I headed that way.

I turned down a grassy pathway toward the grouping of tents where the actors would prep and change during the performances throughout the festival. Most of the plays took place at noon or shortly after, but they pushed the last show —*Pride and Prejudice*—to the evening, after the vendors had all packed up so they could come watch, too. The performance usually lasted until the sun was setting, creating a true feeling of closure to the festivities.

As I moved away from the noise of the main festival, the quiet flutter of the tent canvas and the chatter of rehearsals was peaceful—almost. Parked next to the grouping of tents was one large, completely out-of-place trailer, like the back of a semi-truck.

It didn't need any marking on it to indicate it was Tommy's.

The generator hooked up to it hummed like a perpetual jackhammer, destroying any semblance of tranquility. A group rehearsing to my right kept stopping and yelling, "What?" as they leaned in closer in hopes of hearing one another's lines.

Releasing my frustration through a long breath out my nose, I tried to calm myself. Tommy's loud, garish dressing trailer was a perfect analogy for the impact he'd made in the half day he'd been in Pine Crest.

Covering my ears, I approached the monstrosity, avoiding the door and skirting around until I was standing level with the generator. I was glad Liv had taken Hamburger with her, knowing her reaction to the loud machine would've been a lot worse than mine. It took me a fair bit of searching, but I finally found out how to turn it off. Silence engulfed the field. A few of the actors cheered. I stood up straight and rested my hands on my hips, then walked over to the front. Before I could touch it, the trailer door slammed open. Tommy stuck his head out, coffee in hand, looking right then left until he spotted me.

"Hey," he said. "What gives, Peppy?"

I bristled at the awful name. "Tommy, people are trying to rehearse. Give the generator a break for a while. What can you possibly need electricity for right now, anyway?"

Tommy looked behind him. "A lot. Air-conditioning, my music, and... lights." He said the last word like *duh*.

Scrunching my nose, I tipped my head back and pointed at the sun.

He sighed. "Fine. I don't know how to turn it back on anyway, so I'll have to wait until my assistant gets back from dinner." The door slammed in my face.

Well, at least I'd bought the poor players a few minutes of quiet.

I headed for the biggest tent, where the director usually hung out. There was a white bust of Jane Austen perched atop an ornate pillar, marking the tent as Bonnie's. As I approached, however, I noticed two disadvantages of tents versus a brick-and-mortar building: you could hear everything through the fabric walls, and there was no door to knock on to alert people of your presence.

I stood, frozen, outside the entrance as the angry voices spilled, unimpeded, from inside.

"Calm down, Will. There's nothing we can do about it." Bonnie's voice was still sweet even though it held a definite sharpness.

"Isn't there?" he shot back.

Oh no. This sounded like something I definitely didn't

want to overhear. Grimacing, I stepped forward and cleared my throat. "Hello?" Without waiting for an answer, I thrust my hand through the opening and peeled back the flap.

Bonnie and Will stood in the middle of the sizable tent, posed in a tableau that could've been titled "Dispute." They looked at me, faces flushed.

"Oh! Hi, Pepper." Bonnie raced forward. She was tiny and, from her hair to her personality, the definition of the word *bouncy*. "What can I do for you?"

Tearing my gaze away from Will, who was now pacing in the corner, I met her eyes and I blinked. "Oh, I... just... I wanted to see if you needed anything and..." I couldn't seem to finish. Finally, I broke down and blurted out, "I'm so sorry. I didn't know what to tell those customers. I just remembered you being worried about tickets and... I didn't realize Will was the one playing Darcy."

Bonnie smiled and sandwiched one of my hands in between hers. "Oh, don't worry, Pepper. Thomas put you in an awful position." She sighed, her gaze wandering off for a second. "It's great that we sold more tickets. It just means we have some decisions to make and a little work to do."

"Is there anything I can help with?" I asked.

She refocused her attention on me. After a second, she blinked. "Actually, yes. Would you mind delivering Thomas's script? I need to work on fitting some more rehearsals into our schedule, and..." She swiped a few curls from her forehead, then went over to her desk to grab the stack of papers.

The script? I swallowed a groan and pasted on a smile. *Tommy is going to love this.* "Absolutely," I said as she handed them to me. I grasped the pages and stepped back.

But Will stepped forward. "You seem to know him, Pepper. Think you can convince him to leave?"

Bonnie sighed and went to sit behind her desk, appearing beyond done with this conversation with Will.

"I already told him it wasn't a good idea," I said. "But he had a trailer brought up from California. It looks like he means to stay. Maybe I shouldn't have sold all of those tickets." I looked at the ground.

"No. You did what anyone would do. It's not that big of a deal, really. I'll give up the part. His arrogance is what gets me, though." Will's jaw tightened as he seemed to think. "Walking in here like he owns the place. Hey, maybe we could find something to blackmail him with." He looked to Bonnie. "Everyone in Hollywood has something they're hiding, right?"

At that, Bonnie shot a warning glance over at Will.

His lips moved into a dismissive grin. "Never mind. Don't worry about it, Pepper. We've got a week. We'll figure out a way to get rid of him."

Bonnie cleared her throat.

"Or not," Will added.

There was an animalistic quality to Will's grin, making his teeth appear bared, ready to fight, instead of pulled into a smile.

"Quite the statue you've got out there, Bonnie," I said, trying to change the subject.

She beamed. "Bust, actually. Two feet of real marble. Will got it for me this year for my birthday." She looked lovingly at him.

"Well, I'm sure I'll see you around." I waved, backing out of the tent.

Heading out into the warm summer evening, I gave the marble Jane a quick salute as I walked away. I might have crumpled the pages of the script a little on my walk back to

Tommy's trailer—a small act of rebellion in an otherwise helpless situation.

Standing in front of the trailer, I readied myself to deal with the actor. Before I had a chance to knock on the door, however, a voice caught my attention. I stepped right and saw a blond woman about my age pacing, a phone pressed to her ear. She turned and noticed me, holding up a finger to signal she wouldn't be long. I took a step closer. If this was Tommy's assistant, I would much rather deal with her.

I mean, there was definitely a fifty percent chance she was equally as terrible as him, but—knowing how Tommy treated people—there was also a chance she found him as exhausting as I did.

Hanging up the phone, she walked toward me. "Hi, can I help you?"

"I was looking for Tom—er…Thomas." I reluctantly used his full name. "I'm Pepper." I stuck out my hand.

She took it and we shook. "I'm Karla." She glanced down at her phone when I let go. "Sorry, I'm trying to fix a bit of a mess, and—" She stopped, closing her eyes and shaking her head. "I seriously need a new job." Her cheeks were flushed and she tucked her hair behind one ear.

"How *is* it working for Tommy?" I asked, intrigued.

"Right now? Awful. He's in hot water. Let's just say I doubt anyone will be working for Thomas King after today."

"Why?"

Karla rolled her eyes. "He sent out an open call for a new manager on every social media platform earlier this morning. That person I was talking to on the phone was his *current* manager, the one he didn't bother to give so much as a heads-up that he was looking for new representation."

Cringing, I sucked in a slow breath. "Oh no."

She sighed. "It gets worse. He's coming here—the manager." She pointed to her phone. "That was him telling me he was about to board a plane to Seattle. King may be an ass, but Duncan is definitely one of the scarier men I've ever met. And it sounds like he's out for blood. I'm interested to see how TK slips out of this mess."

"Karla!" Tommy's voice rang out from inside. "Kar-la!"

Glancing up at the trailer, she shook her head. "I'd better go." She winked. "Save yourself, while you can."

I chuckled and skittered away. It wasn't until I was halfway home that I realized I was still clutching the script.

THE NEXT MORNING, Hamburger and I walked over to the festival before I opened the shop. I wanted to drop off the script and end my need to interact with Tommy for good. I saw Bonnie racing around, getting people ready. The next performance wasn't until this afternoon, but I knew she liked to have everything planned out to a T. I waved and jogged over. Hamburger zigzagged in front of me on her leash.

"Morning, Bonnie."

She swiped a loose curl from her forehead. "Oh, Pepper. Hello." Her eyes shifted from one point to another and wouldn't settle on mine. She glanced down at Hammy, who sniffed her shoes and then started growling, backing up a few steps as she did so.

"Is everything okay?" I asked, looking for her assistant, Sarah, who was never far behind. Today, Sarah was nowhere to be seen.

Bonnie's eyes finally met mine. "Okay?" She laughed too loud for a few moments. "Of course! Of course everything is *fine*. Better than." She wrung her hands at her waist, eyes swiveling again.

Pressing my lips together, I pulled in a deep breath. "Well... good. Have you seen Tommy or his assistant this morning?"

"Tommy? Um..."

I nodded. "Thomas King. Or his assistant, Karla. Blonde, twenty-something. I still need to deliver his script." I held up the stack of papers.

Bonnie swallowed and she glanced at the silent trailer to her right. "Right. Um... nope. Haven't seen him yet. Or her." She took a few steps away from me. "I'd better get going. See you around." She spun, curls bouncing in her quick retreat.

My forehead creased in question. *What was that about?* Shaking my head, I led Hammy over to Tommy's awful trailer. The generator was off and I couldn't hear any noise coming from within. I pounded on the door anyway.

Nothing.

Hammy sat in the grass, panting up at me. Ugh. I suddenly wished I'd turned around and gone back to give him the script yesterday when I knew he was in the trailer. I really didn't want to hold on to it any longer, though, so maybe I could just leave it on a table or something. Checking the door, I found it unlocked.

Knowing Tommy wasn't her favorite, I tied Ham's leash to the front of the trailer where there was a patch of shade. "You stay here, girl. I'm going to put this inside." Hamburger flopped onto the cool grass and snorted as she rolled onto her back.

After knocking again, and hearing nothing, again, I gripped the handle and pulled the door open with one hand, holding on to the script with my other.

"Tommy?" I called, placing one cautious foot on the steps and pulling myself up.

Silence.

I walked the rest of the way up the steps and inside until I could see the interior of the trailer. My eyes flicked to the left. Gasping, I stumbled backward, and the stack of papers smacked onto the ground at my feet.

Tommy was sitting slumped forward onto his vanity, a knife sticking out from between his shoulders.

I slammed into the nearest wall. A strangled cry left my lips, but I couldn't look away from him. His head was facing away from me, but I didn't need to see his eyes to know there would be no life left behind them. The dark stain marring his white Darcy costume shirt told me everything I needed to know. My stomach heaved.

I stumbled back out of the trailer and blinked out at the tents of actors and vendors set up nearby.

"Help!" I yelled. "Somebody help!" I pawed at my purse, trying to locate my phone. Panic gripped my throat, making my words sound hoarse as they clawed their way out.

A handful of actors ran over, Bonnie at the head of the group. My eyes locked with hers. "What's wrong?" she asked.

"Someone killed Tommy." The words felt scratchy as they left me, and their terrible taste made me feel nauseous all over again.

"Tommy?" Bonnie's eyes were wide and wild.

I nodded. "Someone stabbed him." As much as I disliked the guy, I hadn't wanted him to die. His personality aside, I remembered the shy, gangly kid who helped my sister with props and backdrops.

Murmurs and gasps blanketed the crowd of actors that

had now gathered. Toward the back, a few people who hadn't been able to hear yelled, "What's happened?"

"Someone's killed Thomas King!"

"Wait. Hold on. What did you just say?" a male voice rang out.

A voice that sent chills down my spine.

I jumped down off the steps and backed away from the trailer as if it were haunted. But the voice hadn't come from the trailer. Tommy pushed his way forward through the crowd. He was wearing jeans and a black T-shirt, not the breeches and puffy white shirt of the costume. The crowd gasped.

"Sorry to disappoint you, but I'm *not* dead, Pepper," he said, rolling his eyes as if this were all an inconvenience.

Eyes wide, mouth open, I looked back at the trailer.

"Then who's in there?"

4

I hurried back inside, wondering if it had been real. Bonnie was right behind me, Tommy a close third. We stopped in our tracks a few feet away from the body. Bonnie gasped slightly at the sight and Tommy swore under his breath.

The person's hand was resting up on the top of the vanity, a ripped piece of paper curled into his lifeless fist. I could see the other hand hanging down by his far side.

Any sense of urgency I felt left me in a flush. The desire to know who it was had been quickly eclipsed by the fear and dread rising in my throat. Tommy stood next to me—let's be honest, he was kind of hiding behind me—his frozen stance mimicking mine. So it was Bonnie who ended up walking the last few steps to peek at the victim's face. I watched her as if she were a mirror and I'd be able to see the identity of the man through her eyes.

All the color seemed to drain out of Bonnie and she wobbled.

"Will," she gasped, then sank to the floor.

My mind raced. *Her husband?* What was Will doing in Tommy's trailer dressed in the Darcy costume?

There was a pain in my chest as I looked at his body. I wanted to go to Bonnie, to comfort her, but I was stuck in place. After what seemed like hours, but was probably only minutes, the wailing of sirens sounded in the distance. Someone must've called the police. The trailer shook and swayed as the paramedics stomped up, pushing past us. Whoever called must not have believed me about the "killed" part. But there was definitely nothing those EMTs would be able to do about the knife cutting through Will's spinal cord at the base of his neck. I felt an arm wrap around my shoulders. Seeing Bonnie was taken care of, I let the person lead me down the steps.

A police cruiser skidded to a stop a few feet away. Frank, Alex's partner, jumped out of the driver's side. My heartbeat slowed a little. Alex wouldn't be far behind. I could definitely use one of his hugs right now. I needed the strength of his arms wrapped around me.

But wait… there were *already* arms around me. In the whirlwind of too many emotions, I hadn't noticed who was holding me. Just as Alex got out of the cruiser, I let my eyes slide to the right to see who I was leaning against.

It was Tommy.

His made-for-TV face was portraying the "upset bystander" character perfectly. He pulled me closer to him. I wanted to push away, but I couldn't seem to find the energy. Alex had already been wearing his serious-cop face, but when he saw me standing with Tommy, his stern features hardened even more. Finding a small store of energy I ducked out from under his arm and walked toward my boyfriend.

"You okay?" Alex's deep voice made my shoulders relax.

A commotion over at the trailer made me turn to watch. Alex's attention followed. A few paramedics led Bonnie down the stairs and away from the crowds. She was sobbing and shaking. I saw Sarah scurry after her and then I looked back at Alex.

"Yeah, I—" I shook my head. "It's Will." I could feel the wheels in my brain working already, trying to figure out how this had happened. Terrible as it sounded, when I'd thought the body was Tommy's, it kinda made sense. I knew I wasn't the only one who disliked the guy. But Will? I didn't see any reason for someone to hate the actor.

Alex's jaw clenched tight as he thought. "Will?"

"He's the one who was supposed to play Darcy," I explained, glancing back at Tommy.

Alex shook his head then looked at the trailer. "I'm going to head in there. You'll be okay out here for a bit?"

I felt an arm slip across my shoulders again. "Don't worry, man. I'll watch over her." Tommy's voice snaked like his arm around me, apparently poking every single one of my boyfriend's buttons.

Alex's brown eyes locked onto Tommy's blue ones. They were pretty similar in height, but whereas Tommy's workout routine seemed to be focused on lean muscle, Alex was built to intimidate. And honestly, as much as I disliked Tommy, I didn't want to see another body today. I shrugged out from under his arm again and stepped closer to Alex. Putting a hand on his chest, I pulled his attention to me.

"I'll be fine. You go figure out who did this." I leaned up and kissed his cheek.

Alex moved quickly and planted a kiss on my lips, then leaned in by my ear, to whisper, "Be careful. I don't trust this guy." His eyes stayed on Tommy the whole time.

I wanted to tell him that I didn't either, but his words

and the icy chill to his tone made my throat close up. Nodding instead, I stepped back as he turned to head into the crime scene.

"Kinda intense boyfriend you got there, Peppy." Tommy stepped closer to me, clucking his tongue as if he were disappointed in me. "Didn't peg him for your type."

My face crumpled in disgust as I looked over at him. "Since when do you know anything about my type?"

He chuckled, dusting nothing off the shoulder of his T-shirt. "I heard you had it bad for me back in high school."

Heat rushed to my face faster than Harry Potter fans to the newest movie. I was going to kill my sister.

"Maggie didn't know what she was talking about." I cleared my throat and looked forward.

"Maggie?" he said. "Naw, Ana told me. She heard a bunch of rumors." His arm was back around me for the third time today. The guy could *not* take a hint.

But my thoughts couldn't focus on escaping from his grasp, they were too busy unpacking what he'd said.

Ana. Of course. Quiet, sweet, almost invisible Ana had been invited to everything. She probably heard a lot.

"Well, whatever," I said. "Things change."

He slid his hand from my shoulder, settling it on my waist. "Yeah they do."

I shoved him away again. "Ugh. *Tommy*. Gross."

Chuckling, he ran a hand through his hair. I could feel his eyes on me. "What? You've grown up... nicely. That's all."

"And you've grown into a creep. A creep who got a nice man killed." I walked away, but I didn't get very far. Tommy grabbed my arm.

"What did you just say?" His forehead was wrinkled in disbelief. "I didn't kill anyone."

I pointed to the trailer. "Tommy, I'm not saying you put the knife in his back, but Will is dead in *your* trailer, wearing the costume *you* were supposed to wear. From the back, you two look very similar. Why do you think I thought it was you at first?"

Tommy's tanned face paled. "You think they were trying to kill me and got the wrong guy?"

I'd figured he would've worked it out already.

"Tommy? Tommy!" The voice stopped me from having to answer his obvious question.

I turned and watched as Ana pushed her way through the crowd. Her eyes were wide and she slammed into her brother, pulling him tightly to her. "I heard—" she couldn't seem to finish her statement, breaking into sobs.

Confusing as it had been to find the body, I was sure the gossip going around the festival was even more convoluted. I could see why his sister had thought the body might've been his.

"Hey, hey." He patted her back. "I'm okay. I'm fine."

I gave Ana and Tommy space and rejoined Hamburger where I'd left her tied to the trailer. She was sitting in the grass, happily snapping at grasshoppers as she watched the commotion around her. I untied her leash and sank down next to her, pulling her close when she climbed into my lap.

After a few minutes, a shadow fell across us. "Hey," Alex said.

Hamburger grunted and wagged her bottom as she moved to greet him, but he remained standing, only reaching down to briefly pat her on the head since he was in uniform.

"Any leads?" I asked, swallowing the uncomfortable heat rising in my throat at the thought of Will's body, of the knife.

He sighed. "Other than the new Mr. Darcy?" He nodded toward Tommy and his sister.

"Tommy? You think he had something to do with this?" I got to my feet so I could hear him better.

"You don't?" Alex asked.

Forehead wrinkling, I said, "Not really. I mean, he's Tommy." I shrugged. "Annoying and terrible, yes, but not a killer."

There was a tightness to Alex's features which was reflected in his tone as he said, "You said you weren't close with him. Maybe he's changed."

I thought about Tommy hitting on me, telling me how much I'd grown. I supposed people could surprise you. "But he seemed as shocked as I was to see it was Will." I blinked. "Plus, he told me he didn't do it." I realized how naive and stupid my words sounded right as they left my mouth.

"Peps, the guy's an actor. He pretends to feel emotions he doesn't feel, for a living. I mean, you said he was good enough to get a part on that show, right?"

"I suppose." I scrunched my nose as I thought. "He's the worst, but he *is* good at what he does." I turned to face Alex. "The thing is… Tommy and Will didn't like each other, sure, but this fight over the Darcy part wasn't bad enough for Tommy to kill Will. I think it's much more likely someone was trying to kill Tommy and got Will instead."

Alex nodded. "That crossed my mind, too."

Frank appeared from the trailer and motioned for Alex to come over. Alex gave my arm a squeeze as he walked away, turning back as he left and saying, "They'll want to ask you some questions if you don't mind sticking around."

"Yeah, no problem," I said, my voice fading as my thoughts took over.

Was I wrong? *Could Tommy really be the killer?* I remembered Tommy and Will's fight in front of the Bittersweet booth yesterday. But Tommy had backed down, the guy was about as tough as well-done spaghetti. Plus, what motive would he have to kill Will? Will had been the one saying all of that "get rid of him" stuff yesterday, talking about blackmail.

Wait. Blackmail.

Now *that* sounded like motive. Had Will found something worth using? Could Tommy have killed Will to keep him quiet?

Just as the thought entered my mind, I saw Karla walk through the crowd, two coffees in hand. Her face was tense and her knuckles white as she gripped the cups, jogging forward when she saw the yellow crime scene tape. I walked toward her.

If anyone would know if Tommy had any skeletons in his closet suitable to be used as blackmail, it was his assistant.

5
———

I wound Hammy's leash around my wrist and walked toward Karla and—

"Ooof!" collided with a solid body.

Hands reached out to steady me and when I looked up, I was gazing into the handsome face of a man in his fifties who looked as if he was posing for a high-budget movie poster. His features wrinkled into a practiced frown which perfectly conveyed the emotion "concerned."

"Whoa there," he said. His voice held the silky-but-still-rugged qualities of a leading man. *Another actor?* I wondered as he flashed a pearly smile at me.

"Sorry, I—" Hammy cut me off with a bark, circling the man's feet and winding him up in her leash. "Oh! Sorry, again." I chased the dog around as the man stepped out from her trap, then I stood once I had her tucked safely under one arm.

Handsome as the man was, my opinion of him dropped significantly as I watched him eye Hammy with annoyance. I was about to turn away from him, but he struck out with a smooth question.

"What's going on around here?"

I blinked, not sure I was supposed to let anyone know about the murder. "I—um—"

Clearly upset at the time I was taking, he said, "It looks as if there's been some sort of crime. Is everyone okay?"

Before I could stumble through another non-sentence, his eyes flashed to his right, locking on something that made momentary surprise turn to a white-hot hatred. It was easy to tell this was not practiced or controlled. I turned to see what the object of his anger was, only to spot…

Tommy.

Face reddening by the second, the man spun away from me and took off. Karla sidled up to me, coffees still in hand.

"You survived meeting Duncan Masters, I see." She shook her head. "What's going on here?"

"Murder," I said, the word a whisper on my lips, a whisper I shouldn't have uttered.

"What?" She turned toward me, but her eyes were frantically searching the crowd instead of on me.

I nodded. "Tommy's fine. That was Duncan?" I blinked as I got my bearings.

Karla took a quick swig of one of the coffees as if it were filled with something stronger than milk and espresso shots. "Yeah. Isn't he the worst?"

"Kinda." I pressed my lips together. "Did he just get in?"

Karla shook her head, straight blond hair whipping from side to side. "He got here last night." Her eyes widened. "He and TK got in a huge fight, and Thomas ended up firing him." Then those same eyes narrowed. "Duncan said he's sticking around to do some fishing, but I think he has ulterior motives for staying in town."

Yeah, like stabbing Tommy in the back. Literally.

Karla and I watched as the police approached Tommy

and Ana. They had notebooks in hand and questions on their lips. Checking alibis, no doubt. But the more I learned, the more certain I was becoming that Tommy had nothing to do with Will's murder, other than being the intended target of that knife.

"Karla," I said, turning to face her. The young woman's features tightening as if she could read my mind, knew my statement before I voiced it. "Tommy's fine now, but I think the person was trying to kill him and got someone else instead."

Her blue eyes flicked over to the trailer and then to her boss, before settling back on me. "I'd like to say it surprises me, but…" Her lips twisted to one side. "Well, you know TK."

I nodded as Tommy looked over and spotted Karla standing next to me. He interrupted the officer who'd been questioning him and snapped his fingers toward Karla. She scuttled over to him then handed over one of the coffees. Chewing on my lip as I thought, I realized I probably shouldn't have told her all of that. If that's how Tommy treated his assistant, she would have a pretty good motive for his murder as well.

My eyes scanned the crowds standing behind the police barricades. Actors had clumped together into small groups. I wasn't sure if it was because of the way they were dressed, in gowns and breeches, or the way people moved from one group to another like a choreographed dance, but it all reminded me of the parties Austen wrote about in her novels. I felt like Elizabeth Bennet, sitting on the sidelines while I watched the locals gossip about the newcomers to Netherfield Park—well, I guess if one of those newcomers had been murdered.

If this was anything like an Austen novel, listening in on

those conversations was going to be the best way to find out information about what had happened.

I picked Hammy up, tucking her under my arm. I skirted around the edges of the groups. Most of them seemed to share Alex's suspicions toward Tommy. Some had tears falling down their cheeks. All seemed completely at a loss about who might have anything against Will.

In the third cluster I approached, I recognized a few women from the Austen productions. Their whispering cut out and the group looked me up and down as if assessing my trustworthiness.

"Hey, Pepper," a girl I knew, named Jenny, said, giving me a smile. She was dressed as a maid and was a few years younger than me, but still seemed to be some sort of leader of the group.

One woman with curly ringlets peeking out from under a white bonnet motioned to the crime scene. "Is what they're saying true?"

"Unfortunately," I said with a sigh. "I can't imagine anyone wanting Will dead."

Most of them nodded, their faces pulled into the appropriate frowns, but a blonde in a simple blue dress cleared her throat. She met Jenny's gaze, but before I had a chance to ask if she thought Tommy had killed him, I caught sight of Alex out of the corner of my eye. He and Frank were standing shoulder to shoulder, scanning the crowd. The frowns on their faces told me they were looking for someone. With my luck, it was me.

Alex stopped when he spotted me, motioning me over. Figured.

"Well," I said. "I better get going." I waved goodbye and then wound my way through the crowd and over to the police officers.

Frank stiffened as he watched me throw one leg then the other over the yellow crime scene tape.

"Hey," I said, tucking a loose strand of hair behind my ear.

"We're ready for your statement," Frank said. He ran a hand up and down his tired face. He'd been on the force a good ten years longer than Alex, but I wasn't sure he'd been the lead on any investigations before this. Alex's dad being gone must've meant he was the lucky runner-up.

"Sure." I nodded and leaned in closer to Alex. "But I think you should start by questioning the man at your two o'clock," I said, turning their gazes on Duncan who was stalking through the groups of people.

"Why?" Frank asked.

"That's Duncan Masters, Tommy's manager. The one he fired last night."

Frank looked at me. "That piece of paper Will was holding was stationary with the initials D.M. on it." The mixture of a detective's curiosity and a Hollywood gossip collector's excitement sparkled behind Frank's eyes. "Pepper, can you wait for those questions?"

"Absolutely. I need to head to the bookshop, but I'll be there if you want to stop by."

Frank told me he would, then went to find Duncan.

Alex turned toward me. "Frank thinks we should cancel the play today. Do you know where they took Bonnie?"

Glancing in the direction she'd disappeared, I pointed. Before Alex could go anywhere, I asked the question that had been on my mind ever since I'd found the body.

"You going to call your dad?" I thought about the quiet and contemplative Detective Valdez and wondered what his take on this whole situation would be.

Alex shook his head. "No. He needs the time away. Plus, we've got this under control."

I nodded. Alex was right. He and Frank could handle it.

"I'm going to go talk to Bonnie. You gonna be okay?" he asked, touching my arm.

"I'll be fine. You go. Good luck."

"Thanks." Alex winked at me. "I'll see if I can stop by later, too. We'll need to touch base about our plans for tomorrow. I'm guessing we're going to have to make a few adjustments. See ya, Hamdog." He gave her a pat and then he headed off to find the newly widowed director.

Hammy and I started for the shop. I should've felt relief the further I got from the crime scene and Will's body, but the opposite was true. The more I thought as we walked, the more my stomach twisted in knots. Or maybe it wasn't about distance, but the fact that—if Tommy really had been the intended victim—this killer may not stop at one body.

By the time I arrived at the bookshop, there was a small group waiting outside. The morning's events had made me a few minutes late. No one seemed to mind all that much, however. They were all clumped together, talking about the body found at the festival. In fact, they almost didn't notice when I finally unlocked the old door and turned the sign to Open.

Pine Crest was saturated with talk of the murder all day, and Brooks' Books was no exception. Customers either spread rumors, gasped at speculations, or asked me about what I'd seen, on a continuous loop until I closed up that evening. It didn't even end when I got home. Liv wanted all the details. Tired as I was, I was craving some Liv and me time, missing our normal chats about boyfriends, life, and our jobs. So, we settled onto the couch and I told her everything.

Literally Gone

THE NEXT MORNING, I woke early—so much so that early riser, Liv, was still in the apartment. While she was sitting in a perfect cross-legged position, it wasn't on a mat in front of the TV following along with one of her yoga routines like most mornings. Today she was on the couch, her laptop balancing on the tops of her knees. And her face didn't look the least bit zen.

"Hey." I slumped next to her, wishing I could fall back asleep on the couch. Hammy jumped in between us. She rubbed her face on the couch cushions and grunted for a few seconds before settling down, too.

"Morning..." Liv angled the computer screen away from me slowly.

I scooted closer to her. "What's up? Whatcha looking at?"

Liv sighed. "I suppose you'll find out sooner or later." She closed the laptop and gave me her serious businesslady look.

"About what?" I tiptoed my fingers over the dog and then along the edge of her laptop, trying to pry it open and see what had her so upset. I'd already told her everything about finding Will's body last night.

Normal Liv would've simply slapped my hand away, but Concerned Liv put her hand over mine, her eyes wrinkled as if I was painful to look at.

I pulled my hand away from her. "What happened?"

Liv grimaced, but opened her computer. "Let's just say, I know one cop who's *not* going to be happy about what Best Entertainment Gossip put as their headlining story today." She turned the screen toward me.

It was some kind of divine intervention I hadn't eaten

anything yet, because as it was I felt like hurling when my eyes took in the picture of me leaning on Tommy, his arms wrapped tightly around me.

The headline read, "King finds a new queen in the midst of scandal."

"Blech!" I pushed the computer back. "Gross *and* incorrect as that is, Alex was there. Tommy was helping me right after we found Will's body."

After I said that, though, questions started lining up in the part of my brain that always legitimately questions if I turned off my curling iron once I've left the house. *Had Alex seen his hand on my waist? Alex knew I was in shock, knew I wasn't actually leaning on him, right?*

Liv sucked in a long breath. "All I know is, in Jane Austen's time, you two would've had to be *very* married in order to let him touch you like that." She paused. "And it doesn't necessarily look like you hate him either, Peps."

I cringed, glancing again at the dreamy look on my face as I stared up at Tommy. "I was still in shock… didn't realize who I was leaning on until it was too late."

There was a knock at the door and Hammy flew off the couch, barking.

Eyes wide, I swatted at Liv. "Quick, put that away. That's Alex."

Sliding her computer onto the table, she glanced at the clock. "You weren't kidding when you said you two were getting an early start today."

"Well, we both have to work later, but I promised him I'd take him somewhere special for, you know…" I glanced at the door and put a hand around my mouth as I whispered, "*her* birthday."

Liv nodded. "Gotcha. Well, I'll get out of your hair." She stood and moved as if to disappear into her bedroom.

"No." I grabbed her arm. "I'm not ready yet. You need to stay here and talk to him so he doesn't look on his phone and see the photo."

Cocking an eyebrow in my direction, Liv said, "Peps, Alex is more likely to show up wearing a tutu than see that article. He doesn't even do social media, and I doubt the man gets his news from any source that has the word 'gossip' in its name. You'll be fine." She rolled her eyes and walked toward her room.

Hammy barked at the door, wagging her body as if she was trying to gather enough momentum to jump up and open the thing herself. Shooting Liv an "I hope you're right" look, I opened the door.

For the past few months, Alex and I had lived in a blissful, beginning-of-our-relationship utopia. So when his face, tight with anger, didn't soften when he saw me, like it normally did, I knew something was wrong.

"Oh, no. You've seen it. Haven't you?" I said, hoping the scrunchy, upset face I was making mirrored how sorry I felt.

Alex didn't say anything, but he walked forward, not even pausing to say hello to Hammy, who was jumping excitedly around his feet.

"And today of all days. I'm so sorry." I shook my head.

Liv, who must've stayed put after seeing his face, chimed in. "Okay, now I'm curious. How *did* you see it, Mr. Off-the-Grid?"

Shoulders pulling up and then dropping in a big sigh, Alex said, "Frank."

Liv and I looked at each other, both shaking a fist in the air as we said, "Frank" through gritted teeth. I should've figured Frank would read all the Hollywood gossip he could get.

"I've got to get my shoes on… that is, if you still want to go." I peeked up at him through apologetic lashes.

Running a hand over his face, Alex nodded. "Of course I do. Today just sucks."

I walked forward. My fingers wrapped around his and I squeezed tight. "I know it does. I'm so sorry." I planted a quick kiss on his lips and then said, "I'll be ready in a jiff."

6

Alex's truck wound up and around the small dirt road that snaked along the ridge of foothills sitting at the base of the Northern Cascade Mountains. Hamburger sat in between the two of us, panting and jumping from Alex's lap over to mine, apparently finding very important things to see out *both* windows. Normally, this would've caused both of us to laugh, but even though Alex had said he understood about the gossip site, it seemed like that picture was still sitting between us.

"Take this right," I said, pointing at a road up ahead.

Cocking an eyebrow at me, Alex clicked on his blinker. "There really aren't any signs?" he bobbed his head as he searched the road for any hint of where I was taking him.

"Nope." I winked. "This is a 'locals only' spot. Unmarked. Just relax, man."

"Okay. I'm trying." Alex sighed and concentrated on the road. Hammy bounded from me over to him, scrambling to gain footing so she could look out the window. "Don't you think it's time for some car training?" he asked as she licked his chin.

"Why?" I chuckled. "This is so entertaining. Plus, I rarely drive. She is a pro at walking on the leash now, though."

"We'll see about that," he said, eyeing her as she jumped back over to me.

I wrapped her up in my arms and glared at him. "Wait until you see her backpack."

Alex scoffed. "What?"

Nodding, I said, "Yup. This little lady's going to carry her own treats and poo bags. She pulls her weight—all fifteen pounds of it."

Hammy snorted as if in agreement.

"Oh, there!" I pointed. "That's it."

Slightly startled by my yelling, Alex slammed on the brakes and skidded to a stop by a rectangular-looking boulder.

"Sorry." I laughed. "It always catches me by surprise. But we're here!"

Alex parked the truck off the road a little more even though I assured him no one really came up this old forest service road.

Hammy sniffed around in the dried grass along the edge of the trailhead while I grabbed my backpack out of the truck bed. Inside was a smaller backpack, which I clipped around Hammy's middle, then spent a few moments chuckling at her as she strutted back-and-forth, looking oh-so-important and adorable as all get out.

I heard Alex's door slam shut and he handed me his keys to stick in my pack after locking the truck. He caught sight of Ham, totally *hamming* it up as she showed off her bag.

He exhaled, shaking his head. "I hate how cute I find that."

Clipping the hip strap on my bag, I laughed. "Don't hate

it, embrace it." I slipped my hand into his, intertwining our fingers. "Ready?" I looked over at him.

"I'd follow you two anywhere."

I smiled. It seemed as if he was finally letting go. "Good answer." I pulled him after me as I started up the trail. I was determined to get him to have a better day, upset I'd been one of the reasons it had started off poorly.

Hammy jogged ahead, tongue lolling, the little saddlebags on her pack shifting from side to side with each step. We didn't talk much for the first few minutes. The air was the perfect temperature and the quiet sounds of nature filled in all of the space around us like that expanding foam spray insulation. Birds chirped, branches swayed in the breeze, and the mountains seemed to hum around us. I could feel my shoulders drop and Alex's gait lengthen as we both let go of the emotional baggage we'd brought with us, focusing purely on the physical.

The hike wasn't anything difficult. The forest road had brought us most of the way up the small mountain, so it was mostly flat for the mile walk along a tree-crowded ridge to our destination. There was actually a road that led all the way up to the destination vista—forged mostly by the Joshua brothers and their giant trucks—but it was slightly treacherous. Plus, I loved a good hike when I could fit one in.

The terrain was a little rough at times, since this wasn't one of the National Park's maintained trails, but it was a worthy trade given the solitude it afforded. Which was what Alex had said he wanted today. Today, the day his mother *would've* turned another year older. Knowing how tough it was for me on my father's birthdays, I had asked Alex what he felt like doing.

Even though I'd been totally prepared to honor his wishes if he wanted to be alone, he'd surprised me by saying he wanted to hang out with me. Just me. Right when he said it, I knew where to take him. Maggie and I had come here on Dad's first birthday after his passing. There was something about being reminded how small and insignificant you are that helped put things like grief and life into perspective —or at least, I thought so.

I hoped Alex would appreciate it, too.

We began to chat about our favorite memories of our parents, laughing and taking a few silent moments whenever we needed to. Soon the trees began to thin and the blue sky opened up in front of us. Squeezing Alex's hand, I pulled him forward the last hundred feet. Hammy had already beat us and was barking as she skirted the water's edge. When we cleared the last few trees, and I heard Alex's sharp intake of breath, I knew I'd made the right decision.

Tearing his gaze from the turquoise-blue glacial lake and the valley we were now looking out over, Alex turned to me.

A smile tugged at the corner of one side of his mouth. There was a sadness hiding behind his eyes, but I'd expected that. It was the peace I saw smoothing out the rest of his features that truly felt like a thank you.

"Peps, I—"

Before he could finish what he was going to say, my phone began buzzing in my backpack. I was surprised I even had service out here in the woods, but I tried to ignore it, looking up at Alex. The buzzing stopped and I smiled. "Sorry, what were you say—"

I was interrupted by more buzzing.

"Just answer it," Alex said, chuckling.

Pulling off my pack, I fished out my phone, holding it in between us so I could read the name. I didn't recognize the number, which normally meant I didn't answer, but with the events of yesterday, I figured it could be important. I answered it.

"Hello?"

"Pepper, it's Thomas King." His voice rang loudly from the speaker, causing me to pull the phone away from my ear slightly.

My eyes flicked up to Alex's. He had definitely heard.

"What do you want, Tommy?" Features hardening, I wished I hadn't answered.

"You know how you said the killer was trying to get me? I—"

Interrupting him, I said, "Tommy, I don't have time for this right now. Sorry." I ended the call, then turned the phone off as I walked over to Alex where he stood looking out on the valley. "Sorry, I don't know how he got my number."

Alex shook his head.

"I'm serious!" I said, grabbing a hold of his arm. "Please. I don't know what you think, but the guy is the last thing I want to come between us."

His shoulders slumped. "I know. I'm sorry. Okay, what did you have planned out here?"

"Follow me." I smiled.

After slipping off our shoes, we splashed our feet in the glacial lake. Once our toes were officially frigid, we leaned against some boulders and pulled out our books. I produced a bag of trail mix I'd packed. Happy snacking and reading commenced. At the end of each page, I stopped to look around, glancing at Hammy to make sure she wasn't swallowing any pieces of the stick she was chewing on or gazing for a moment at the summer sunlight shining on the blue water.

Alex and I held our books with one hand, our free hands

meeting in the space between us, fingers intertwined. He was still reading his slightly-rumpled copy of *Pride and Prejudice* and I had brought along my own Austen. In my hand was a pretty special, antique hardback copy of *Persuasion* I'd splurged on when I found it in a book seller's online catalog last month.

When the sun was almost directly above our heads, we started packing up, preparing to head back to reality. We were supposed to have the whole day off, but with the murder yesterday, Alex could only take half of today. Maggie was watching the shop for me, so I figured I'd relieve her early. I placed the Italian lace bookmark Dad had gotten me for my eighteenth birthday into the hardback and closed it gently while Alex folded down a page and tossed his book into the open backpack next to me. Chuckling—because it was easier than yelling at the guy—I stood and stretched.

"Ooh," I said, hands moving to my lower back. "Boulders are not the most ergonomic of surfaces."

Alex rubbed his butt as he stood. "Nope." He closed the space between us. "But the view's worth the pain." His arms wrapped around me as he pulled me tight to him and pressed his lips against mine. "Thank you for bringing me here, mi pimienta," he said as he pulled away, using his Spanish nickname for me, *my pepper*.

I nodded, not quite trusting my voice as my throat grew hot with emotion.

We tucked Hammy's stick into her backpack so she could take it home with her, and packed the rest of what we'd brought into mine.

"Before we go," I said, giving him a wink. "There's one more thing we have to do."

Alex lifted his eyebrows with intrigue as I led him over to

the big boulder overlooking the lush valley. Hammy wisely stayed back, guarding our things. I scrambled up its craggy side and then scooted closer and closer to the edge until my legs dangled over the precipice. Alex followed, a final sigh lifting his chest and then settling as he peered over the edge.

"This boulder has the best view," I said, explaining even though Alex seemed to understand why we needed to come up here before we left.

It felt like we were the only two people in the world—well, three if we counted Hammy, which I did. Until, that is, I looked down. The Joshua Brothers' makeshift trail snaked up the hillside, passing right under the boulder before climbing all the way up to the lake. The two cars were parked below us. One was an older, black sedan. The other a new, red one.

"Huh," I said, tipping my head for a better look. "That's odd."

Alex caught sight of what I'd noticed. "Wait, we could've driven all the way up here?" he asked, nudging me with an elbow to show me he was joking.

But I didn't feel like joking. I looked around us, bobbing my head up and down, side to side as I looked for anyone. The cars appeared to be empty and we hadn't seen nor heard anyone else the hour we'd been here.

"That's super weird." My forehead wrinkled together as I thought.

"Maybe they came up here for some privacy and we've ruined their time," Alex said, getting up. "Speaking of time…" He set a hand on my shoulder. "We're almost out of it."

It had been a popular make-out spot for members of the Pine Crest High student body, but it was the middle of the day. But short of hiking down there and peeking into the windows, there wasn't much I could do to solve the mystery. I got to my feet and scrambled back down the boulder. There was an odd, nagging feeling in the back of my mind almost the whole hike back to the car.

Eventually, Hammy's backpack antics and Alex's hand wrapped around mine tugged me back into the present. Alex tossed our stuff in the back of the pickup and lifted Hammy into the cab, her dusty paw prints collecting on the cloth of his seats as she pranced around.

But as we headed down the mountain, I couldn't help but stare at the fork in the road that led back up to the lake and wonder once more about the two cars mysteriously parked up there. Pulling out my phone to distract me, I turned it back on. A groan rose in my throat as I saw seven missed calls from the same number.

Tommy.

7

After grabbing a quick sandwich to go from Bittersweet, Hammy and I headed to the shop. The fact that I'd had to get my sister to watch the shop reminded me that I really needed to hire a part-time employee to help me run the place, especially when I started grad school in the fall. I added it to my long list of things to do as I entered the shop.

"Hey," I said, smiling at Maggie as she waved from behind the counter. Hammy gave her own, gruntier greeting as my sister scratched her ears.

I sighed and looked contentedly around the warm, dusty, sunlit space. I loved watching people as they walked through the shop. Their faces relaxed, eyes shining as they viewed the book-filled shelves and tables. And as much as a bookshop was a treat for the eyes, people couldn't seem to help running their fingers ever-so-lightly along the bindings, along the gilded and sometimes rough edges of the pages. Hands would linger on a shelf as they cocked their heads to the side to better read the titles, and fingers would grasp a book they couldn't live without tight to their chest as they continued to look.

Hammy made three passes through the place upon our arrival and then flopped onto her bed with a sigh.

Most of the time, the store seemed to bring a hush upon a person. But every once in a while we had a talkative group or a small child who was too excited to contain their exclamations. Brooks' Books seemed to be full of the chatty sort.

"Murdered?" one lady asked, as she picked up a beautiful copy of *Sense and Sensibility* from the Austen table.

Her companion nodded. "That's why they've postponed some of the shows, it was the director's husband." She leaned closer to her friend. "Plus, there's a murderer on the loose."

Glancing at Maggie, we gave each other knowing looks. It wasn't only these customers who were scared, the whole town was reeling. People had started a memorial for Will at the fountain in the center of Pine Crest, placing flowers, pictures, and cards as tears dripped down their faces.

"How was your morning?" she asked when I made my way behind the register with her.

Pushing the odd feeling about the two cars out of my mind, I focused on Alex's smile and how relaxed he'd looked by the time we'd headed home. "Really good. Thank you so much for watching the place for me."

Maggie bumped me with her shoulder. "Anytime. Josh wanted to take the kids to the park anyway and I'm happy to get a break. But you probably shouldn't tell Mom I was here," she added.

"Oh, good thinking." I nodded.

Mom had commented many times about how I needed to hire someone instead of closing when I had to leave or getting family to watch the place.

My mother had actually purchased the shop for me when the previous owner had put it up for sale at the beginning of the summer. I was paying her back—slowly but surely. This was a big step for the two of us. Up until that year, my mother and I had always had a difficult relationship—I'd always been so much more like my messy, literary-loving father. After he died, the rift between my mom and me only seemed to widen. But we'd been working on it and everything was slowly getting better. In fact, this whole "hire a part-time employee" bit was the only thing Mom had stuck her nose into, shop-wise, since she'd helped me buy the place.

Which meant I should probably listen.

But before I could say anything more, the front door opened as the bell above it announced a new customer. Maggie's face tightened in recognition for a fraction of a second.

Excited whispers filled the shop. I turned around to see Tommy standing behind me, his hair mussed in a way which —for once—didn't look like he'd gelled it that way on purpose. Even his posture seemed scrunched down, a shadow of his egotistical self. His attention darted around, then settled on me.

Hamburger growled from where she lay in her bed, but apparently didn't see him as enough of a threat to stand up.

"Hey, Tommy…" I said, sharing Hammy's suspicion.

"Pepper." He dipped his head in a hello, hair falling into his face as he sent nervous glances over each shoulder. Then, for what seemed like the first time, his eyes met Maggie's. "Mags?" He walked forward, seemingly genuinely excited to see my sister.

"Hi, Tommy. It's good to see you," she said. Her face softened, but I knew from the way her lips pressed together for the briefest of moments, that she was lying. Their time together had been pretty short and was years behind her, but it didn't mean she wanted to rehash an old, failed relationship.

Tommy's eyes swept over her. "You look great." He glanced at me, apparently agreeing with my loud—and awkward—exclamations about my sister's body from the other day.

Maggie blinked and then said, "Uh. You, too." I could tell she regretted it the moment she said it.

Tommy pushed back his shoulders and winked at her. "Thanks."

I scoffed, but my sister kept her feelings hidden this time. She was much too sweet sometimes, reminding me of the kind and gentle Jane Bennet. I was glad she had Josh and was no longer susceptible to getting her heart broken by this man.

"Pepper, can I talk with you?" Tommy said, gesturing to the right with a tip of his head.

I looked at Maggie to make sure she didn't mind manning the counter for a few more minutes. She waved me away with a flick of her hand and I followed Tommy over to the reading nook, situated in the bay window at the front of the shop.

My fingers ran across the cover of a copy of *The Complete Works of Jane Austen*. Happy to see the stack considerably smaller than before, I was glad I'd decided to add the title to my most recent order.

"You have *one* minute," I said, straightening the stack.

Even though Alex and I had worked things out, Tommy's phone call in the middle of our date today had definitely *not* made the tension between us any better.

Tommy's wild eyes met mine. "I found something."

My scowl dropped away. "What? Why didn't you tell me earlier?"

"You didn't give me a chance."

He was right. I hadn't. I wrinkled my face into an apology as I asked, "What is it?"

Looking right and then left, Tommy reached into his pocket. He produced a slightly crumpled piece of paper.

"This was stuck under my windshield wiper this morning." He handed it to me.

The words, *"Watch your back"* were penned across it in a slanted script.

"Whoa," I blinked at the harsh words then looked up at Tommy. "This was on your windshield?"

He nodded, swallowing slowly.

"Tommy, you need to show this to the police."

His face tightened. "I was afraid you were going to say that."

"Why? They might be able to help."

Tommy shook his head. "I'm pretty sure I'm at the top of their suspect list. What if they use this as evidence against me?"

"They're simply looking into all suspects," I said, handing the paper back to him. "If you have nothing to hide, you're fine turning this in." I watched my words sink in.

Finally, Tommy folded the paper, stuck it back in his pocket and nodded. "Yeah, you're right."

All of this talk of suspects had made me curious again, however. I asked, "Can you think of anyone who might be mad enough at you to resort to murder?"

Normal, cocky, not-scared-out-of-his-wits Tommy probably would've scoffed and given me some offhand remark about how everyone loved him. But this was someone-who-looked-like-me-was-murdered-in-my-trailer Tommy, and his face immediately scrunched together in thought.

"Duncan, I guess." He met my eyes. "My manager—well, ex-manager."

"Right." I knew the police were already looking into him.

"The guy was pretty upset the other day. I mean he flew all the way up here all over a stupid post on social media, one I didn't even make."

Tipping my head to the side, I asked, "You didn't?" I remembered Karla telling me Tommy had very publicly announced how he was looking for new management.

Tommy shook his head. "No. And I told him, but he wouldn't believe me. Said he has screenshots of the post, but when I went to look it wasn't there." He shrugged. "I mean, I suppose you could make most anything with Photoshop these days. Maybe someone's trying to mess with him. Regardless, the guy flew off the handle. It's why I fired him. I just can't handle drama like that in my life."

Stifling a gag at Tommy's clichéd statement, I asked, "And is losing you as a client a big enough deal to him to kill over?"

Tommy scoffed. "Of course. I'm his biggest client."

Unable to know if that was really true, I decided to remind Alex to look into it. "Anyone else?" I asked.

Tommy raked his fingers through his hair and chuckled. "There are a few ex-girlfriends who I'm pretty sure hate me enough to bury a knife in my back." His eyes flicked to Maggie. I was about to tell the guy he was officially on his own if he suspected my sweet sister, when he added, "But none of them are around here."

I tapped my fingertips along the table next to me as I thought, noticing I needed to dust yet again. The underappreciated and overworked assistant finally losing it and offing the awful boss story wasn't a new one. As much as I liked—and empathized—with Karla, I couldn't forget her words from the other day. "*I doubt anyone will be working for Thomas King after today*." Had it been more about the fact that firing his manager was a bad career move or had she been foreshadowing something much more sinister?

"What about Karla?" I asked.

Tommy scoffed. "Karla? The girl worships me." His head whipped from side to side. "Naw. She—" he cut out, a frown marring his features for a moment before he resumed shaking his head. I hoped a few of the scenes like the ones running through my mind at that moment, were running through his as well, though I had no doubt what I had witnessed was far from the worst.

I heard the bell over the door announce a new customer. I turned to greet them, but stopped short, seeing my mother enter.

A groan escaped me. I saw Maggie duck behind the counter. Unfortunately, Mom had already spotted her. Mom's eyes flicked between my sister and me. The woman was a lawyer and so even when she was dressed down in jeans and a T-shirt she was intimidating. But in her full heels and power suits getup, the woman was downright frightening. Especially with how stiff her posture was. Especially when I knew it meant she was disappointed in me.

Tommy pushed his shoulders back. "Mrs. Brooks." He dipped his head in a hello.

"Thomas." The way her eyebrow arched told me she was slightly annoyed with his presence.

"How are you?" Tommy asked.

"Better than you, I hear," she said, keeping her eyes focused on me.

Mom was a rational businesswoman, but she was also a fully entrenched Pine Crest resident, which meant she knew all of the gossip.

At the reminder of his predicament, Tommy cleared his throat. "Uh, how's your—how's Mr. Brooks?" He scanned the place, probably hoping to catch a glimpse of my father, wishing for some relief from Mom's viper-like stare.

My dad, contrary to popular stereotypes, had always been the more accepting parent when it came to our boyfriends. He was laidback and jovial, often getting too attached to the guys only to learn we had broken up with them, or they with us. And while I can safely say Tommy had *not* been someone Dad had formed a particularly strong connection with, I understood the guy's preference.

The problem was, Dad was gone.

My mother's smooth, in-control facade faltered, and I knew she was feeling the same, stabbing pain of loss at the mention of Dad. After two years, it was definitely more of a dull, resounding ache than the sharp spike of pain it used to be when he'd first passed away, but it was still there, nonetheless.

"He passed away a few years ago," Mom said, pain making her words sound as tight as my lungs felt.

Tommy's face fell in a way that I was certain—like his hair—was not practiced or on purpose. I appreciated how upset he looked about the news.

Having had enough of her conversation with Tommy, Mom sighed, turning her attention to me. "Honey, you *really* need to hire someone." She pointed over at Maggie. "Your sister won't be able to cover for you once Josh's schedule gets busier in the fall, not to mention *your* schedule."

"I know, Mom. It's been crazy around here and this is a small town. There aren't a ton of unemployed people looking for part-time job opportunities. If I wait until closer to fall quarter, Pine Crest will be full of university students wanting work."

Tommy raised an eyebrow. "My sister's looking for work."

I blinked. "Ana? But isn't she like…" I suddenly drew a giant blank on what classically trained pianists fresh out of Juilliard did for a living, so I finished with, "… leaving soon?"

"She's taking a break from music for a bit." He smiled in a distinct, "I don't want to talk about why" kinda way.

"Oh." It wasn't the most thoughtful statement, but I was too busy with all of the reactions running through my mind. On one hand, Ana was perfect. She was sweet, great with people, had a great smile, and loved books. On the other, she and I had never really gotten along in school and I wasn't sure how working together would… work. It wasn't like we were enemies or anything, just never close friends. But she had seemed different at the festival the other day. "Uh, are you sure she'd want part time?" I asked warily.

Tommy said, "Sure, she wants to give piano lessons on the side, too."

Mom cleared her throat. "See, Pepper? Perfect." She straightened her lapels and walked over to say hello to my sister.

Still a little surprised by my luck, I turned to Tommy. "Can you tell her to come by when she can and we'll do an interview?"

He said he would and then turned to leave.

"And stop by the police station." I widened my eyes at him to show him how serious I was.

"Will do. Thanks, Peppy." He winked.

Stiffening at the sound of the awful nickname, I joined my mother and sister at the register.

Mom smiled as I approached. "Oh, I've changed our dinner reservation tonight for three people instead of two."

I blinked and looked to my sister. "Is Maggie coming with?"

Honestly, I didn't mind if my sister wanted to come. Mom and I had started our Sunday night dinners as a way to get closer—only the two of us—but we were doing much better lately.

Maggie shook her head. "Not me. I've got a hot date with some chicken nuggets."

Mom smiled. "I was thinking it's about time I got to know Alex better. I've already called him and he accepted the invitation."

8

"Yeah, she called me earlier. I hope it's okay I said yes," Alex explained when I called him after Mom and Maggie left the shop.

The hope in his voice made a heavy layer of guilt settle over me. Alex had been wanting to get together with my mother for a month now, but I'd done my best to postpone the event.

"Sure. It'll be great," I said, hoping it sounded like I actually believed it.

It wasn't like I had been *keeping* Alex from my mother—but I definitely had been *protecting* him from her. The woman put every boyfriend Maggie or I had through what we called The Interrogation. And it wasn't like I thought Alex couldn't hold his own with my intimidating mother, but that didn't mean it wasn't going to be awkward as all get out.

"Pick me up at six?" I asked, feeling a resigned sense of acceptance.

"You got it. I'll be the one in the tie," he said and I hung up with a smile on my face.

This was going to be fine. Alex was the first cop I'd

dated. And cops pretty much invented interrogations, right? Still, my anxiety grew the closer I got to dinner.

After closing up the shop, Hammy and I walked home, arriving at the apartment at five thirty. As I unclipped Hammy's leash, my worried eyes settled on Liv and her boyfriend, Carson, sitting on the couch as they watched a movie. His messy brown hair was the perfect contrast to her perfectly styled blond bob. Drastically different, the two of them just worked.

"What's up?" Liv asked, pausing the movie.

My friend could read my distress all too well.

"Oh—haha—nothing. Except Mom invited Alex to dinner with us tonight." I said, picking at something on my nail that wasn't really there.

Liv sat up. "The Interrogation?"

Gulping, I nodded.

"He'll be okay. Right?" She tipped her head uncertainly.

"He'll be here in a half hour. That's the only thing I know right now." I shrugged. At this point, things were out of my hands. I headed toward my room, Hammy following at my heels. "I'm gonna change real quick," I added before closing my door.

I spent the next nineteen minutes trying on practically every piece of clothing I owned, searching for something nice, but didn't look like I was trying too hard. Eventually, I settled on a cream-colored summer dress spotted with bright green flowers which was equally comfortable as it was cute. Liv had insisted I get it last year because it went so well with my auburn hair. Plus, it had pockets. How much more unassuming could you get than a dress with pockets?

I held my breath as I heard Alex knock on the door, early as usual. After a quick swipe of a brush through my hair, Hammy and I left the sanctuary of my room. Stuffing my hands into the pockets of my dress, I sauntered into the living room, cool as a cucumber.

Until my eyes landed on Alex. His hair was swept back and he had just enough stubble to look completely irresistible—I'd started to call it his eleven o'clock shadow. The man was wearing a dark-gray button-up with a light-gray tie that highlighted his tanned skin, making him look like a Latin movie star. He had the sleeves rolled up a few times—because it was summer for goodness' sake—and had completed the look with a pair of jeans, making me quite sure he'd gone through the whole nice-but-not-too-nice dilemma in his head, too.

It wasn't like I had forgotten, but my boyfriend was *hot*.

I heard snapping to my right. My eyes flicked over to Liv as she looked between the two of us. "Peps, I think you've got a little drool going there, and, Alex, pick your jaw up off the floor."

My cheeks grew hot and I glanced at the floor, then up at Alex. I suppose I hadn't been the only one ogling. He walked over to me and held out his hand.

After placing my hand in his, I said, "Sorry," after noticing how sweaty my palm was, comparatively. "It's possible I'm a little more nervous about this than I let on."

Alex let go of my hand so he could wrap me up in his arms. "Everything is going to be fine," he said, leaning close and whispering in my ear. "I'm super likable. Relax." He kissed my cheek and I just about melted.

Liv added, "Bring us some tiramisu, would you?"

I laughed. "You got it."

We headed for the door.

"Good luck, you two," Carson called.

I hoped we wouldn't need it.

Mom had picked a place called Yum Rosetti, a Vietnamese-Italian fusion restaurant. Normally walking into the building made me sigh and take a deep breath of the spicy, garlicky loveliness. Today, I clutched Alex's arm, not able to smell anything but fear due to my shallow breathing.

"Pepper!" Mai Nguyen, one of the owners, called as we entered. While born in Vietnam, the woman had grown up in Chicago, so the thick accent she sported was Illinois, through and through.

I smiled weakly and waved.

Mai smiled at Alex and then said, "Your mother is already here, Pepper." She waved for us to follow her.

Pausing, I looked up at Alex, who nodded. "Everything's going to be fine," he repeated.

We followed Mai back to the table where my mother waited. Now that my dad wasn't around anymore, she tended to work on weekends. Her dress shirt, slacks, and suit jacket hanging on the back of her chair told me today was no exception.

When she saw us, Mom stood, wearing a huge smile—something she definitely didn't usually wear when she was litigating… or interrogating. Knowing what was coming, however, made me feel like it was all a trap.

"Alex. It's so nice we could finally do this." She pulled him into a quick hug, then grabbed me. "I love this dress on you, honey." She beamed at me, tucking my hair behind my ear like she always did when I was a kid.

We sat down and opened up our menus. Before I could even begin to narrow down the myriad of choices, Mom started into The Interrogation.

"So, Alex. How do you like being a police officer?" she peered at him from over her menu.

I sighed.

Alex smiled. "I like it a lot. Both my mother and father are—er—were." He cleared his throat.

I knew the awful, stabby feeling he was experiencing in that moment, having to correct himself, having to use *were*.

Mom's face softened from warden to widow, remembering how I'd told her his mom had been killed in action. "Right. And is your father liking it in Pine Crest?"

Alex nodded. "We were looking for something small and boring, though, I think we overestimated the boring part."

I snorted. That was the understatement of the year.

"Pepper, what have I told you about snorting?" Mom scolded.

"To not do it." I rolled my eyes.

"And rolling your eyes?"

Sighing, I said, "Mo-om."

Ugh, Alex was coming off looking great and I was regressing into a whiny teenager.

But then Mom turned back to Alex and asked, "Don't you worry about it being so dangerous, though? I mean, no offense, but aren't you worried something like what happened to your mother could happen to your father… or you?"

My heart stopped. *She didn't…* I shot my mother a sharp look of warning, but she didn't take her eyes off Alex, who hadn't paled or balked at the question in the least.

He dipped his head in a nod. "Of course. It's a dangerous job. I grew up never knowing if my parents would make it home after a shift. But even after one of them didn't, I'm still proud of the difference she made, the difference my father and I can still make."

Mom reached forward, placing a hand over one of Alex's for a moment. "Of course you are." But she wasn't a successful lawyer for nothing. The woman obviously hadn't gotten the answer she was looking for, so she kept going. "Are you willing to put your own children through the same worry and heartbreak you went through?"

Kids? She'd never brought up kids at an interrogation before. I wanted to crawl under the table.

"Mom, he's not on the witness stand. Cool it." I widened my eyes at her.

But Alex took hold of my hand and simply said, "I'm not in a place in my life where I'm thinking about kids—just yet—but, yeah. Absolutely. Life is full of heartache and joy. It's all about the balance. The person my mom was—my dad is—and the person they raised me to be, it's all a direct result of their career choice. I know I cherish the time I spent with my mother and appreciate still having my father around. I think a lot of people take things for granted if they don't know loss." At this, he reached under the table and laced his fingers through mine, squeezing tight, telling me he knew I felt the same way.

Lip tugging up slightly in one corner, I nodded. "Yeah, I mean, we lost Dad and he didn't have a dangerous job at all. You never know."

Mom, always rational, accepted my reasoning and smiled back at me. "Very true."

My shoulders slumped forward slightly in relief. Past experience told me we had made it through the worst of The Interrogation.

"So if you're not thinking of children right now, what are you thinking of?" Mom asked right as I let my guard down.

Okay, she was basically asking Alex what his intentions

were with me. Had we been transported back to Miss Austen's time along with the festival? I felt like Elizabeth, sitting helplessly by as Mrs. Bennet asked every single man whether or not they thought she was marriage material.

My eyes slid to watch Alex, itching to tell him he didn't need to answer her question. But as with every difficult question before this, the guy was ready.

Alex grinned. "I think of Pepper, mostly." He glanced over at me, winking.

I glanced down at my lap and smiled. Okay, I still felt the urge to crawl under the table, but now I wanted to bring him with me.

My mother, for the first time in a long time, was speechless.

He continued. "I think about how she has a literary reference for every possible situation and I'm constantly wondering which one she's going to use whenever something new happens. I think about how she's equally as kindhearted as she is intelligent. I think about what a great friend she is, what a great family member."

At that, he looked over at me. Then he chuckled.

"I think a lot about how to keep her out of the trouble she always seems to find herself in. And I think about how lucky I am."

Mom's lips had slowly pulled into a smile while Alex talked—after she got over her surprise, of course. She winked at me, then said, "Good answer."

My heart was beating too fast for me to focus on anything but Alex's hand holding mine. *Yeah. A really good answer*, I thought, blinking down at the menu for something to take my mind off how flushed my face must've been.

"And beyond Pepper?" She cocked an eyebrow.

"I like to write when I get the chance. Poetry mostly, but I've started a few stories."

I turned to look at him. "What? I didn't know that." How had I not known that about him?

Alex smiled. "I was a little intimidated to show you, to be honest. You're such a literature buff. I wasn't sure if you would like it."

"Of course I'll like it." I could hear the anger at being caught so off guard cropping up in my tone, so I added a soft, "Whenever you're ready to show me, that is. No rush."

"So you think you two have a future together? Past the summer?" Mom asked, proving beyond a shadow of doubt she was insatiable in her quest for knowledge—or that she was seriously trying to ruin my life.

I automatically broke into a cold sweat at the question. Alex and I hadn't been together long enough to have any sort of discussion about our future. And I really didn't want our first discussion about it to be in front of my mother.

Luckily, before Alex could say anything, Mrs. Nguyen led someone else to a table nearby. Someone who caught my attention.

Tommy's manager, Duncan.

My panicked brain saw an opportunity—like a drowning rat attempting to cling to the slippery sides of a bucket—futile as it might seem.

I popped out of my seat and waved. "Duncan. Hey, over here. Why don't you join us?"

Duncan might be just what I needed to avoid any more questions from Mom. Plus, I might also be able to get a few of my own in at the same time. Even though joining us appeared to be the last thing Duncan wanted to do, Mrs. Nguyen smiled and brought him over.

"Oh, how lovely." The small woman set the extra menu

down onto the table next to my mother, who looked up at the man, still mostly stunned at the turn of events. "I'll be right back for your orders," Mai said, pouring Duncan a glass of water to match ours.

"Thank you," Mom said, then turned to Duncan again. "Hello, I'm Lillian, Pepper's mother." She held out her hand.

Duncan's handsome face seemed to light up as his gaze settled on my mom. "Duncan Masters."

"And how do you know my daughter?"

"He's Tommy's manager, Mom. We met the other day."

"Ex-manager," Duncan said.

Mom laughed. "Oh, well good riddance, I say. That boy is nothing but trouble."

Duncan's lips pulled into the first smile I'd seen him wear. "I'll drink to that," he said, picking up his water and clinking it with my mother's.

Alex sat back, but instead of wearing his meeting-your-mom, friendly boyfriend face, he'd switched over to his impossible-to-read, serious-cop face. Hmm… maybe we both would get something out of this.

9

By the time our orders showed up in front of us, I completely regretted inviting Duncan over.

Sure, his presence had officially stopped The Interrogation, but it seemed like—dare I say it?—it seemed as if my mother was... flirting.

Duncan was a good-looking older man, that was for sure. I'd almost mistaken him for another actor the first time I'd seen him, after all. But the man was most likely a murderer, and my mother was all over him like words on a page.

I poked at my food, and when Mom giggled—actually giggled—I officially gave up on eating. Alex, on the other hand, was eating as if he hadn't done so in about a month.

My stomach churned as I watched the terrible scene in front of me grow worse by the second. I glanced over at Alex, regret written over every inch of my expression. But he was paying too much attention to his food. I sighed and turned my attention back to Mom and Duncan.

"Terrible business." Duncan shook his head.

"I know." Mom shook her head, spearing a shrimp on

her plate and popping it into her mouth. "Did you hear Pepper found the body?"

Duncan's eyebrows rose. "I hadn't heard that." He looked over at me. "It must've been quite the terrible surprise."

Lips pressed together tightly, I thought, *No thanks to you. Maybe next time you kill someone, make sure you've got the right guy first.* I kept those words inside, however. Instead, saying, "Yeah. It was pretty awful." I sipped at my water and moved more food around on my plate. "It's a good thing you weren't around when it happened. I mean, where were you?"

Mom laughed. "Oh, honey. He was probably far away from that mess."

Duncan nodded, shooting me a smile so fake it made my teeth hurt. "Yeah, exactly. I was grabbing a coffee at that Bittersweet place when we all heard." He shook his head. "Nasty business."

Alex stiffened next to me. The police were probably still working to corroborate his alibi. I exhaled the hopes I'd had of catching Duncan off guard and decided to entertain the idea that maybe Duncan wasn't the sure-thing suspect I'd thought he was. Mom was usually a pretty astute judge of character, too, so if she liked Duncan, maybe he wasn't so bad.

As I thought through the other possible suspects, I began to eat some of my meal. Could it really have been Karla?

"Have you ever done any acting yourself? Or have you always been a manager?" Mom asked, blinking dreamy eyes at the man.

He chuckled and flashed those bright white teeth in a movie-star smile. "It's how I got into the business in the first place. People always said I looked like an actor. But I tried and I'm pretty much garbage at hiding my emotions. I can't even play poker. My friends say they can even tell what suit I have based on my face."

Mom laughed along with him. "So do you usually come along with your clients when they travel?" she asked.

Duncan shook his head. "Not usually. Especially since Thomas has Karla. No." His eyes shifted from her to his plate. "To be honest, whenever Thomas has talked about his hometown, it's always sounded so idyllic to me. I've thought about visiting for a while now. But I just had my fifty-fifth birthday last week and I guess it's hitting me that all I've done is work, work, work for all of my life. I needed a break, a little getaway." Duncan shrugged. "Maybe do a little fishing. I don't know. I needed to get out of the city."

And to threaten Tommy for firing you, I added in my thoughts, knowing Duncan wasn't going to admit the real—and less flattering—reason he was in town.

My mother sighed. "Tell me about it. Getting older makes you look at everything differently." She laughed. "Heck, fishing is even starting to sound kind of wonderful. My late husband used to love to fish. If you need any equipment while you're here, let me know."

I chuckled to myself, knowing Dad's idea of fishing was propping up a fishing pole in a boat while he floated around the lake reading, completely undisturbed by my schedule-making mother. He never caught a single fish in his whole life.

Duncan smiled. "That's okay. I've actually recently acquired my own fishing paraphernalia. But you'd be a welcome guest, if you want to bring along your set. Do we need licenses in this state?"

"Oh, probably, but we've never purchased any." Mom waved a dismissive hand at Duncan, then covered her mouth with her hand quickly and looked at Alex. "Oh, gosh. I probably shouldn't say things like that in front of you, Alex." Mom gave me an apologetic smile from across the table. She leaned closer to Duncan. "Alex is part of the local law enforcement."

"Oh? That's—I would definitely make sure we had the correct permits, of course." Duncan cleared his throat and dabbed at his mouth with a napkin.

I looked to Alex, hoping he would ease this poor man's worries with a good-natured wave at my mother and a laugh. But he only nodded, staring down Duncan. From the tension gathering by the second at our table, it almost felt like I was in the middle of some Austen-esque feud.

And true to Austen feuds, this one wasn't going to be easily resolved. Duncan turned and caught Mai's attention as she walked by.

"Ma'am, I'm ready for my check, please." He placed his napkin over his plate, still mostly full of food.

Mai paused, glancing at his plate and then up at the rest of us. "Oh, did you not enjoy it?"

"It was wonderful. I just remembered I have somewhere to be. Thank you."

"Oh. I thought…" Mom blinked. "Well, it was great to meet you."

"Yes. Great." Duncan, having been all smiles and charm for the past half hour, seemed almost cagey in his switch. He seemed to catch himself, facing Mom after he signed his bill. "It was nice to meet you, Lillian." He took Mom's hand briefly before standing up. "I'm so sorry I have to go, but I would love to see you again, if time allows during my visit." After a quick kiss to her knuckles, he handed her a card.

And then he was gone.

"That was odd," Mom said, finally, frowning at the rest

of her food, looking very clearly as if she'd lost her appetite. "I thought we were having such a nice conversation."

"Yeah," Alex said in that cop way that meant I couldn't read into what it meant, at all.

We picked at our food and sipped at our drinks for a few more awkward moments before Mom asked Mai for our check.

Flabbergasted as I was, it took a lot more than that to make me forget about dessert. "Two orders of the tiramisu to go, please?" I added before she could leave.

Minutes later, clutching the desserts, Mom, Alex, and I wandered outside.

"Thanks for dinner, Mrs. Brooks," Alex said.

Mom blinked, her attention returning to us. "Oh, you're very welcome." She held her hand toward Alex. "I hope we can do this again." They shook, Alex nodding in agreement.

I balked at the thought, still scarred at having to witness my mother on what seemed increasingly like a first date.

Mom pulled me into a tight hug. "Love you, honey." She stepped back and then headed toward her car.

After saying goodbye to my mom, Alex and I walked to his truck. We sat inside the quiet car for a good few moments before either of us got our thoughts in order.

"Pepper," Alex said, turning toward me. "Your mother has to stay away from him."

I blinked. "Oh…kay. Yeah, I mean it's super weird to see her interested in someone other than my dad, but it's been a few—"

"No." Alex started the engine and pulled out of the parking lot. "That's not what I mean. Duncan was a person of interest in this case before, but I think he just gave me enough evidence to bring him in." His eyes were focused on the road, but his lips twitched every few seconds like they always did when he was thinking through evidence.

"Seriously?"

Alex nodded, his Adam's apple bobbing as he swallowed. "You don't think it was completely bizarre how quickly he changed and then practically ran out of there?"

I tipped my head from side to side. "Well… yeah, but I figured he's really intimidated by cops and got nervous about my mother's criminal past, fishing without a proper license." I chuckled as Alex pulled into the parking lot of my apartment complex and turned off the car.

But Alex didn't laugh. "The alibi he gave us tonight was different from the one he told Frank the other day," he said, pulling out his phone.

I blinked. "What?"

"He told Frank he was drinking coffee."

"And?" He'd said he was at Bittersweet. I didn't see what Alex was getting so worked up about.

"In his hotel room at the inn," Alex finally added. "Duncan said he has a room facing the park and came to see what happened when he saw the police swarming Tommy's trailer." Alex shook his head, focusing on his phone for a moment. He sent a quick text, which I couldn't read, but I did see Frank's name at the top of the screen.

"What?" I clutched the seat. "Oh gosh. Seriously? Then… then that means my mom was flirting with a *murderer*." I swallowed slowly. "And if Duncan has already killed a man, why wouldn't he go back for the real target?"

Glancing down at his phone for a second, Alex furrowed his brow.

When he didn't respond, I said, "I mean, Tommy's in real danger here, Alex."

Alex exhaled sharply, pulling away from me. "And what

if Tommy is the killer, trying to cover his crime by making himself out to be the victim?"

"But you just said Duncan…" I threw up my hands.

"We can have more than one suspect, Pepper. Tommy's still at the top of our list. I know he showed you the piece of paper he said he found on his windshield this morning." Alex lifted his eyebrows.

"So?" I held his gaze.

"The piece of paper with the threat is the same one that was ripped out of Will's hand."

I blinked, remembering the section of paper grasped in Will's hand when we'd found him.

"Omigosh!" I leaned closer. "Frank said it had something about Duncan's stationary on the top. Which means Duncan had meant for the victim to be Tommy."

Alex bobbed his head. "Maybe. But there's still the possibility Tommy wrote it to threaten Will and tried to rip it out of his hand. He could've made up the part where he found it on his windshield."

I closed my eyes for a second. "I don't know, Alex. I don't think Tommy's guilty."

"Why? Because you know him so well?"

Scoffing, I said, "No, I'm trying to look at all of the facts instead of letting my emotions get in the way like you."

He let his head fall back. "Just because I don't like the guy doesn't mean I'm trying to falsely accuse him of murder. The victim was found in his trailer, they'd fought the day before, Tommy's alibi is shaky—at best—and you said Will mentioned how he was going to try to dig up dirt on the guy. You're right, I don't like him. But that doesn't mean I'm going to let him get killed, if he was the intended victim. You need to trust me."

"So I need to trust you, but you won't trust me?" I shook my head.

Before Alex could respond, his phone rang in his hand. I saw Frank's name flash across the screen.

"Look, I gotta take this. You'll be okay getting inside?"

Nodding, I slipped out of the truck as he answered Frank's call.

"Yeah, I'm on my way," he said, turning the car back on and putting it into reverse.

Alex's eyes met mine for a second before I closed the door behind me and headed toward my apartment. I looked back as he pulled out of the lot, feeling altogether too much like Elizabeth Bennet thinking sourly of the rude Mr. Darcy after their first interaction.

"I could easily forgive his pride, if he had not mortified mine."

10

Liv and Carson looked up expectantly as I entered the apartment after Alex left.

Setting my purse down, I knelt to hug Hamburger as she trotted over to say hi. After a few good scratches, she squirmed away. I flopped face-first onto the floor—making sure not to crush the tiramisu I'd brought in with me.

"Oh no, Peps," Liv said, chuckling lightly. "That bad?"

"Worse," I said into the carpet, the word muffled. I peeled myself up and picked lint from my lip. "We need to vacuum more."

Liv shot me a withering look.

I groaned and stood up, handing Liv the dessert. "Alex and I just got in a weird fight. I don't really want to talk about it just yet. Plus, I gotta call my mom and tell her she can't see the man she flirted with at dinner tonight anymore because he's most likely a murderer."

Giving Liv and Carson a half-hearted salute—and ignoring their confused expressions—I headed into my room where I was *"free to think and be wretched"* just like Elinor Dashwood.

After sitting on my bed for a few minutes, head in my hands, I called Mom.

"Hey, Pepper. What's up?" Mom sounded breezy, happy like I hadn't heard her sound in years.

Cringing, I said, "Mom, I need to talk to you about Duncan."

"Honey, I know it must be hard to see me have fun with someone other than your father. It was weird for me too. But I really connected with him."

This was going to be tougher than I thought. I sighed. "Mom, you can't see him anymore."

She laughed, the unamused one she reserved for our teenage years when we said ridiculous things like "I'm boycotting household chores," or "You're ruining my life."

"Pepper, it's not like you to be so dramatic about something like this. I'm sorry, but it's been two years since your dad passed away. Do you expect me to live the rest of my life alone?" she asked.

"No. I'm fine with you dating if you find the right guy, it's—"

"Well, thank you *so* much for your permission," she said, interrupting me. "And if you don't mind, I will make the decision about who is right or wrong for me." Lawyer Mom had shown up. Without needing to see her, I knew she had pushed her shoulders back and raised her eyebrows. "Good night, Pepper."

She hung up.

"And now Mom's mad at me too," I grumbled to myself, then headed out of my room to drown my sorrows in coffee-flavored cream and cake.

Liv had put a slice of the cake on a plate for me, a fork at the ready.

"Have I told you lately that I love you?" I said over my

shoulder and grabbed the plate before padding into the living room.

Liv winked at me as I slumped into the armchair next to the couch and then sank my fork into the tiramisu.

"How'd the phone call go?" she asked, pausing the movie they'd been watching.

Scrunching up my nose, I stuck the first bite into my mouth. "Not well," I said around a mouthful of cake.

"So since when is your mom into murderers?" Carson asked.

"Since I invited one to eat dinner with us after Mom started questioning Alex, and I got all panicky."

Carson nodded as if it made sense to him.

"And this murderer is?" Liv asked.

"Duncan Masters, Tommy's ex-manager."

Met with blank stares from both Liv and Carson, I filled them in on the theory Tommy had been the intended victim, and therefore was still in grave danger. Liv always had a way of making me see things differently, and Carson, laid back and funny as he was, had a sharp mind. I waited, looking forward to hearing what they thought of it all.

"If that's the case, the killer has to be either Duncan or Karla." Carson squinted as he looked at the ceiling, thinking through what I'd told them.

I nodded. "Or Bonnie. I mean, she was happy about selling more tickets, but he really made her job a lot more difficult." As I said the reason aloud, I realized how flimsy it sounded as a motive, so I added, "And that morning, she was super awkward when I ran into her before heading over to the trailer."

"But that means Bonnie accidentally killed her own husband instead of Tommy," Liv said, shaking her head. "I don't buy it. She would've known the difference between her husband and someone else. I mean, I'd recognize the back of Carson, and we're not even married.

Carson waggled his eyebrows. "Would you now? Spend a lot of time looking at the *back* of me?"

Liv elbowed him. "Oh, come on. You know what I mean." She chuckled, despite efforts to remain serious.

"You have a point." I tapped my fingers against my lips as I thought. "I think it has to be Duncan then."

Liv cringed. "Sounds like it. Which means you really have to get your mom to listen to you."

I nodded. "I'll have to talk to her in person. I can go tomorrow before I open the shop."

There was a terrible feeling in the pit of my stomach which only grew as I thought about talking with mom and the evidence stacking against Duncan. Sinking my fork into the tiramisu, I almost didn't feel like eating another bite. Almost.

"Mom, you can't see Duncan anymore."

I took a deep breath.

"Hey, Mom. A funny thing about Duncan is he killed a guy."

Shaking my head, I tried again.

"Mom, maybe don't get too attached to Duncan since he's probably going to prison for murder and won't be able to date for a while."

Hamburger panted as she looked up at me. We were walking to the bookstore the next morning and I was practicing breaking the news to my stubborn mother.

"Hammy, you wanna try telling her instead of me?"

The dog looked away, sniffing something on the sidewalk to avoid the question.

"Figures," I mumbled as we approached Nate's coffee shop, Bittersweet.

Sitting right inside the café, was my mother. With Duncan. I froze, feeling a momentary bout of frustration rise up in me. *After I'd told her not to see him?* Hammy kept walking, unaware I'd stopped and she was yanked back when she reached the end of her leash.

"Sorry, girl," I said, leaning down to pat her as I watched my mother laugh and beam at the man across from her.

Just then, she glanced out the window and saw me, waving and—if I was seeing clearly—turning a little red like a child being caught with an extra cookie they shouldn't have taken.

I pasted on my best accepting-daughter smile and waved back, then motioned for her to come outside. I held up one finger to show her I only needed to talk to her for a minute and then gestured toward Hammy with a shrug, letting her know I couldn't bring the dog inside.

Mom said something to Duncan, who turned and looked at me over his shoulder. I tried to look happy and calm as I waved at him too, feigning normalcy so he might not suspect anything. Finally, a sigh of relief washed through me as I watched Mom get up and walk outside. She smiled and greeted Hammy, standing and giving me a questioning look.

But before I could even open my mouth, tires screeched to a stop behind me and car doors slammed shut.

Whirling around, I watched Alex and Frank leave their cruiser parked along the sidewalk as they headed for the door of the coffee shop. Alex gave me a look about as informative as a paper bag. Hammy recognized Alex and started to trot over to him, but I pulled her back toward me, pretty sure I knew what was about to happen.

Mom blinked and watched them enter the coffee shop. They stopped in front of the window, talking to Duncan. We couldn't hear what they were saying, but it was one of those scenes you don't need words to infer what was happening. When they clasped the handcuffs over Duncan's wrists behind his back, it was all pretty clear.

To everyone except my mother.

"Wait! What are they doing?" Her wild eyes met mine, and she flinched as if stung by my lack of surprise. "You knew about this?"

I nodded, then shook my head. "Well, the part where he was a suspect, yes. Not how they were going to arrest him this morning." I put a hand on her arm. "Sorry, Mom."

I thought about how Duncan had the best motive out of anyone—other than Will—to kill Tommy. Then there was the threatening note, written on Duncan's stationary, left partly in Will's hand and partly on Tommy's windshield. Alone it hadn't been enough for a warrant, but his lying about his alibi seemed to be the final piece they'd needed.

Her mouth hung open as she watched the scene in the coffee shop, then her eyes slowly returned to me. She pulled away, shaking her head. "No. This isn't right. Duncan's not… he can't be." Her hand rose to cover her mouth and she watched Alex and Frank escort Duncan out of the café.

Frank was reading the man his rights as they walked past us.

Mom strode forward. "Alex, I demand to know what is going on here."

When he sighed and said, "Mrs. Brooks, I'm sorry." My

mom turned back to Duncan, who met her with an equally worried look of his own.

"Lillian, please believe me. I didn't do this." He tripped slightly, trying to walk sideways while his hands were still cuffed behind his back.

Mom blinked while Frank opened the back of the police car and pushed Duncan inside. I reached out and grabbed her hand, tugging her toward me, gently.

"I was trying to tell you last night," I whispered, supporting her. "I'm sorry. I didn't know they'd gotten a warrant already."

The police cruiser pulled away. A chill crept into my gut as I saw a pale expression cross my mother's face, a whisper of the one I'd seen the day we'd learned of Dad's heart attack, but unsettling still. She shook her head.

"I know it's irrational and I know I've only met him twice…" Mom petered out. I'm sure the rational, lawyer part of her was unwilling to let her finish her statement.

My hand rubbed her back like she used to do for Maggie and me when we had bad dreams. "I know, Mom."

Spinning to face me, she seemed to find a store of energy. Or was it hope? "I can represent him. I can show them the evidence isn't there." Her brown eyes flashed across my face, reading my reaction to her idea.

I couldn't bear to look. Glancing down, I shook my head.

"The evidence is definitely there, Mom. I don't even think a lawyer as good as you is going to be able to help him now."

11

The town was completely abuzz the rest of the day. Mom eventually calmed down enough to go to her office, so Hammy and I opened the bookshop, only to hear various—and mostly untrue—retellings of the arrest spill from customers' lips throughout the day.

Among the intrigue, however, there was also a fair amount of excitement. With a suspect behind bars, people felt safe again. The festival had remained open, but attendance had suffered considerably after Will's murder. Bonnie's assistant Sarah had taken over the remaining directing so Bonnie could focus on preparing for Will's funeral, but I'd heard the show the day after the murder was poorly attended and gloomy. Knowing justice had been served seemed to make everyone feel at ease.

So when Karla showed up at the bookstore the next morning, holding a bottle of wine complete with a bow, she had to skirt around the crowds of people picking up a book or a souvenir before the festival opened that morning.

"Hey." I tipped my head in a greeting as I rung up an older couple who stood with their hands clasped together, whispering excitedly about trying the Meryton Meals meat pies for lunch today.

Karla smiled and gestured that she would wait until I had a free moment. The festival opened in ten minutes, so I knew things would begin to clear out any second. Fifteen minutes later, the shop was all but dead. I sighed, swiped the back of my hand across my forehead, and walked over to where Karla sat in the window seat, flipping through a copy of *Emma*. I plopped down next to her.

She set down the book and proffered the bottle of wine toward me. "A thank you from Thomas King." She snorted. "For keeping his butt alive, apparently."

I eyed the bottle and put it down next to me. It was, without a doubt, something wildly overpriced and overrated —this was Tommy we were talking about.

"Um... Thanks?" We looked at each other and laughed. "I didn't really do anything, though."

Karla shook her head. "Yeah, I know. It's really me who deserves the wine, but TK doesn't see it that way."

I leaned in closer. "You deserve it? Why?"

"I was the one who gave the police the final piece of evidence that helped them get the arrest warrant." She picked at something on the bench seat.

"Which was?" I asked.

Karla sighed, as if she'd had to tell this story a thousand times already. "Well, as you know, Thomas's trailer was completely closed off after the murder and we couldn't get in there. They finally finished with their fingerprinting and inventorying and all that jazz, two nights ago. Mr. King refused to go in, which left me."

I snorted. "Sounds like Tommy."

Rolling her eyes, she nodded. "I had to get a few items—

mostly hair products," she added in a murmur, "from the trailer. When I went in there, I noticed the box of fishing supplies Duncan had asked me to buy for him sitting on the counter. But after a quick scan of the contents, I could tell right away the knife he'd asked me to buy was missing. Don't ask me why you'd need a knife to go fishing in the first place, but…"

"Guts," I said.

She nodded. "Thank you. It was nighttime, but I didn't want to turn the generator on, so I was only equipped with the flashlight on my phone."

"No." I chuckled at the city-girl's misunderstanding. "I mean, you were brave, but the knife was for cleaning the fish's guts out. If you gut a fish right away it stays fresh a lot longer."

"Oh." Karla blinked. "Sure. Anyway, the knife was missing. The one *Duncan* had asked me to buy for him. The police wouldn't say, but I'm sure it's the one used for the murder. The whole fishing thing must've been a ruse so I would buy him a knife." She huffed. "He was probably going to try to pin it on me."

I chewed on my bottom lip. "Yeah, maybe." Though I couldn't help but feel a pang of worry at the thought that Duncan hadn't tried to pin it on anyone. And he hadn't gone back after Tommy. It could've been because the police were on high alert, but something felt off.

"Anyway." Karla stood up. "I'd better get back to the grind."

"Sure you don't want a part-time job at a bookshop instead?" I asked, mostly jokingly.

Karla laughed. "Oh, I could never live anywhere other than L.A., honestly. Even though it would be way easier to live here on the salary Tommy pays me." Her eyes narrowed. "I can barely afford my closet of an apartment, let alone food."

The air between us turned awkward after her complaint. Attempting to keep things light, I waved a hand at her and said, "No worries. Just thought I'd ask. Tommy said Ana might be interested, anyway, so there's that." I smiled.

Karla's face darkened for a split second. "Oh?"

Tipping my head, I asked, "She's not your favorite, is she?"

The woman shrugged. "She's so ungrateful. I mean, Thomas paid her tuition to that hoity-toity school, and she goes off and throws it all away." From Karla's tone, her feelings toward Tommy's little sister were more than clear.

I knew a lot of people who were taking a little time off between graduation and starting their careers, so I felt like Karla was being a bit harsh saying she was throwing her education away by doing so, but I wasn't in the mood to argue.

"Sorry," she said, obviously seeing the worry on my face. "I'm just missing home, so I'm cranky. She'll be great in here." She winked and turned to leave.

"Hey, Karla?" I needed to check something. I'd gotten an itching feeling at the back of my mind and I needed to scratch it.

She stopped. "Yeah."

"Is Tommy sticking around to play Darcy then?"

"He is." She twirled a finger in the air. "For the fans."

I laughed. "Make sure you post something on Pine Crest's Facebook page so people know." I pressed my lips together for a moment. "Do you need me to add you to the group?"

Karla waved her hand toward me. "Naw. I use TK's account and I know he's part of that group."

"Okay. Cool."

I watched her go. When she was out of sight, I grabbed my phone out of my pocket and texted Alex.

> Please stop by if you get a minute. Bad feeling.

IT WASN'T until lunchtime that my surly, sleep-deprived boyfriend sauntered into Brooks' Books.

His broodingly handsome disposition reminded me of the iconic Mr. Darcy from *Pride and Prejudice*. *"Darcy was clever. He was at the same time haughty, reserved, and fastidious, and his manners, though well-bred, were not inviting."*

Yup. Not-inviting was Alex's middle name these days—well, actually, it was Herbert, which always made me giggle—but I was seriously thinking the guy should consider changing it. Between this investigation and his mom's birthday, the poor guy was dealing with a lot. As much as I felt for him, I was beginning to understand Elizabeth Bennet and her frustration with Darcy's churlish attitude toward everything a little too well.

Hamburger ran over to greet him, apparently unaware of his sour state. Of course, he picked her up and then let her lick his chin for a few seconds, cracking the first smile I'd seen him make in a while. He scratched behind her ears before setting her down and then patted off the white fur she'd left behind on his black uniform.

"Hi," I said, bright and cheery, hoping to capitalize on the good mood Hammy had gotten him into. I walked up and slipped my arms around him.

Alex sighed and folded over me, pulling me close. "Hey."

He sank his chin onto the top of my head and I breathed in his soapy, clean, Alex smell.

"Sorry we fought." I snuggled closer.

"Me too." His chest rose and fell in a deep breath.

"Rough day?" I asked.

He nodded.

I pulled him tighter and let him relax for a few moments.

"Would you be mad if I had to make it a teensy bit more complicated?" I kept myself tucked safely under his chin, too worried to come out yet.

But I didn't need to look up to know his reaction. I could feel it as he stiffened.

"Your bad feeling." His words were resigned, like someone standing in front of an insurmountable hill, knowing the struggle about to befall them.

"Yeah," I said, finally meeting his gaze as I stepped back. "I'm not saying you should let Duncan go…" I bit my lip and worked up the courage to say the next part. "It's—well—I think there's cause to keep looking, is all."

"I thought you were convinced it *was* Duncan," he said.

I nodded. "But then I had a very enlightening chat with Karla this morning that I think you'll be interested in."

Alex let his head drop forward, his hand swiping across his stubbly chin and working its way up his face. "What did she say?"

Grabbing his hand and giving it a quick squeeze, I said, "Let's start from the beginning. What is Duncan saying about his alibi? Why did he lie?"

"Well, now we have a third alibi. First it was having coffee in his hotel room, then it was coffee at Bittersweet, and now he's saying he lied because he really *was* at the trailer. He was looking for Tommy, wanted to apologize since they got in a fight the night before. He couldn't find Tommy, so he left to walk around town for a bit. When he came back, he was surprised to find everything blocked off. Sounds pretty convenient to us, plus the fact it's his third take at it."

"Did he go into the trailer the first time?" I asked.

Alex recognized where I was going with my question and shook his head. "He says he didn't. If he's telling the truth, that means Will could've already been dead inside. But the coroner placed time of death at just a few hours before you found him, so that also puts Duncan at the crime scene during that window. He could still be lying."

I clasped my fingers together, squeezing them tight as things began to click in my mind. "But don't you remember Duncan telling us how he hadn't made it as an actor because he's terrible at it? I mean, he said he couldn't even play poker."

Alex shrugged. "Perfect cover story, I'd say."

"But he didn't even know you were a cop when he said that." I paused. "And remember how crazy and nervous he acted when he found out about your job? He knew he'd been caught in a lie with his alibi."

Alex opened his hands. "Yeah. Pepper, you're only proving how guilty the guy is."

"No. I'm proving he might *not* be. He couldn't hide his worry, left in a hot mess right after he found out. That doesn't seem like a criminal mastermind to me."

"Seems like a desperate man, mad enough to stab a client in the back because he thinks he's been fired, messy."

Sucking in a slow, deep breath, I tried not to let Alex's doubt sway me. "But now add in Karla. She's hiding something." I thought back to the bad feeling I'd gotten after talking with her. "The reason Duncan came up here in the first place was because he was worried Tommy was going to fire him. And what caused the man to believe that?"

"A post on social media?" Alex asked, squinting one eye as he tried to remember.

"Yes. And does Tommy look like a man who makes his own posts on social media?"

Alex cocked an eyebrow at me, incredulous.

Right. He had a point. If social media was a person, it would be Tommy. He embodied the self-absorbed sites.

"Okay, different question. Would a guy who asks his assistant to pluck his eyebrow hairs miss the chance to have her post all of his pictures and updates?"

He bobbed his head in concession.

"Karla has access to his account. Duncan saw a post Tommy said he didn't write and when they looked again, it was gone. What if Karla posted it and then took it down?"

Alex scoffed. "Sure. But why?"

I hadn't completely figured that part out yet, but I had an idea. "To lure Duncan up here."

"Okay." Alex sighed. "Let's say she did."

"And she happens to be the one who bought the knife," I added.

"That Duncan asked her to buy." Alex pointed out.

"Alex, the dude called it 'fishing paraphernalia' at dinner last night. That man is the last person who would know you need a knife to gut the fish. Karla's the one who made the decision to buy the knife. I think she may have framed Duncan. She was complaining about how little Tommy pays her and then mentioned how much he spent on Ana's tuition. I think it's possible she finally got fed up with her working conditions."

Nodding, Alex walked over to the bench seat in the

window and sat down. I could tell by the way his brows were knit together that he was listening, though, so I kept going.

"And the night before Will's murder she said something really cryptic about how no one would be working for Thomas King for much longer when I asked her how she liked her job."

Alex shrugged. "Okay, that sounds like motive, but she was at the coffee shop when it happened."

"Was she?" I asked, sitting next to him.

"We're still waiting on a few people to confirm her alibi." Alex looked at me. "But I'd be lying if I said she wasn't on our radar. Someone did send both Frank and me an interesting email earlier." He pulled out his phone, tapping the screen for a few seconds before holding it out in front of me.

A video took up the display as he tipped it to the side, making the picture bigger. It was a little wobbly at first, but once it steadied, it was easy to make out Tommy and Karla sitting at a table in a quiet restaurant. From the streetlights and glowing signs visible out the window behind them, you could see it was nighttime.

"You're going to regret this," Karla said, spitting the words out like a bad taste.

Tommy's hand shot forward and he grabbed her wrist. "What are *you* going to do about it?"

"I'm going to make you pay. When you're least expecting it, I'll come for you." Karla's eyes narrowed into slits. "And believe me, I'll make sure you can never hurt anyone else like you've hurt m—"

There was a loud noise and Karla stopped, looking over her shoulder. They watched something for a moment and then turned back to face each other. The video stopped.

Alex slipped his phone back in his pocket. "The emailer

was anonymous, but they obviously think Karla had motive to kill Tommy. And, I don't know, with a threat like... What?"

I winced.

"You think this is something?" he asked.

Shaking my head, I said, "Oh, it's *something*, but it's not a death threat."

"How do you know?"

That was the part I *really* didn't want to have to admit. "That was just someone catching Karla going through Tommy's lines with him for his show. I may have watched an episode… or two, in the past."

Alex's eyes crinkled at the corners like they did when he was trying not to laugh. "Seriously?" He let out a deep, rumbly laugh. "Okay, that's kinda funny."

I wrinkled my nose as he kept chuckling. "Look, it's a dumb show, but sometimes things like that suck you in, and it's so dramatic, I—"

"That's okay, Peps." He winked. "I won't tell anyone your secret." His lips pressed into a thin line, a sure sign he was suppressing more laughter.

"Laugh it up, you. But there's something not too funny about all of this."

He waited, giving me space to speak.

"Whoever sent you the video is either unaware of the context or they're trying to plant fake clues to throw you off the real ones."

Alex cleared his throat. "Right. Which begs the question, which of the clues are real and which aren't?"

12

Alex headed back to the station to share with Frank what I'd told him about the video clue they'd gotten. In the meantime, I got ready for my interview with Ana.

I'm not sure if it was me who'd changed since high school or if it was Ana, but she seemed to have developed a lot more personality. After fifteen minutes, I ended up hiring her on the spot. She said she could start immediately.

Already, having an employee was turning into the best thing ever. After teaching her how to use the computer system and giving her a quick tour, I'd cleaned out my office and gone over the inventory directions Simon, the old owner, had left for me knowing I would need to start that soon. I lugged one last box of books from the office out to the register, having left Ana alone for probably too long on her first day. I could look through the books out front.

She smiled as I emerged from the back. There weren't currently any customers and she was dusting. Hammy trotted alongside me, having followed me back to the office earlier to sleep in the bed I kept for her in there.

"How's it going?" I asked.

"Great." She beamed.

Setting down the box near the register, I flipped open the top and began pulling out books. Most of them were from my dad's library and would be finding a home on my personal bookshelf in the office, but I'd come across a few personal novels I'd already read many times and didn't mind putting up for sale on the used book shelf. Finding one such book, I started a "sale" pile and a "keep" pile.

"You look like you're still moving in," Ana said, brushing the duster over the front windowpanes.

"There are so many jobs I just couldn't ever get done when I was the only one here. You're a lifesaver, really." I shook my head. "I still can't believe you brought in your favorite books as your resume."

Ana giggled. "Worked, didn't it?"

I nodded. "Like a charm."

She'd shown up with an arm full of books and a smile on her face.

Turning back to the box in front of me, I found something for which I would need to start a third pile. Or burn. My fingers traced over the cracked binding and the bright-pink flower sticker I'd wrapped around it. An old diary.

"Find a treasure?" Ana stepped forward.

"More like trash." I laughed. "It's my diary from…" I flipped through a few of the pages, eyes scanning entries. "When I was about fifteen, I'd guess."

"Ooh. Juicy. Anything good?" She raised her eyebrows.

Paging through, I groaned. "If by juicy, you mean mortifying, then yes." I stopped on an entry, catching Tommy's name in the text. "Ugh. This page I'm talking about when I had a huge crush on your brother."

Ana giggled, but gave me my space.

"I sound like a total stalker." I furrowed my forehead.

"Holy smokes, listen to this, *If I can't have him, I don't want anyone to have him.* Talk about crazy."

"I'm pretty sure I have a dozen diary entries that sound just like yours. I liked the older guys too." She waved a hand toward me. "Don't worry about it."

Interest piqued, I asked, "Older guys? Who?" Ana had been so quiet during high school, apparently resisting the urge to share her crushes with everyone who possessed ears like the rest of us.

Her cheeks turned slightly pink. "The Joshua brothers."

Our eyes met, and we broke into belly laughs.

"I never pegged you for someone who liked bad boys," I said after our laughing had subsided slightly.

Ana smiled and shrugged. She didn't seem to want to talk about it, though, so I went back to my box, taking the last of the books out to sort. Then I took the "keep" pile back to my office, along with the incriminating diary. I placed the diary in the bottom drawer of my desk, not sure I was ready to burn it just yet. I was certain I didn't want anyone getting a hold of it, though. Embarrassing as it would be, with Tommy an intended victim in a murder, it could also make me look like a suspect.

The last thing on my list checked off, I headed back up front. Hammy must've gotten used to Ana already, because she had stayed up front with her and was watching her as she finished washing the front window. That taken care of, I turned to the computer, looking at the sales totals for the day so far, while Ana put away the cleaning supplies and moved on to reorganizing the Jane Austen table.

"This is cute." She picked up a small, plastic bust of Lady Jane, turning it in her hand.

"Nothing compared to the one Bonnie has at the festival. Have you seen it?"

Ana's eyes went wide as she nodded. "Real marble."

I laughed. Bonnie must tell everyone she can. "Yeah, Will gave it—" I cut out, having forgotten how the rest of Bonnie's bust speech was a lot less endearing now Will was dead.

Ana gulped.

"Ugh," I groaned. "I keep forgetting."

Busying herself with the merchandise on the table, Ana nodded. "Me too."

Wishing I hadn't killed our good mood, I tried to change the subject. "So Tommy said you wanted to take some time off now that you're done with school. What are you going to do after that?"

"Honestly?" Ana finally looked up from the books. When she saw she had my attention, she continued. "I don't really know. There's a lot of pressure for me to use my degree. I still love playing the piano, but I think I may have burnt myself out a little in the last few years."

Being someone who'd only recently decided what I wanted to do with my life, I got her indecision. "You think you'll ever go back to New York?"

Ana lifted a delicate shoulder and let it fall. "Probably. I needed to come home for a little bit, where everyone knows me. You know how that is? In New York it was so easy to be someone else, not like here where everyone's known you your whole life. I used to hate it. It's part of why I left. Funny how that's all I want right now. I came home because I think I forgot who I was. The moment I stepped foot back in Pine Crest, I was surrounded by people who knew me and reminded me who I was."

I nodded. Living in a small community could be grounding for some people, but equally intimidating for others. I was about to share my own struggle to find out who

I was, who I wanted to be after I'd lost my dad, when I noticed Ana staring out the shop windows, a darkness I'd not noticed before marring her usually pristine features. It startled me a bit, honestly, and I decided to leave her to her thoughts. Before I could look away, Ana's gaze met mine, and her face returned to its default smile, leaving me with the impression that the darkness was something she worked to keep hidden. I returned the gesture, but quickly busied myself with today's numbers.

After that, a mildly uncomfortable silence settled over the shop as we worked, so I was happy when we were interrupted by the bell over the door ringing, and I saw Nate Newton striding into the shop. Hammy, who had been snuffling under a chair in the corner—she liked to chase the dust bunnies around, snapping and barking at them—ran over to greet the new customer.

"Why hello there, juicy little burger." Nate bent forward in a bow, tipping an invisible hat at her.

Ham cocked her head to the side, part of her lip caught in her teeth, and blinked back at him. Nate's word choice was creepy at best, and while I know I was technically the one who had a dog named after food, it always worried me a little when he referred to her as such. Or maybe it was how he tacked on the word *juicy*. I tried to paste on a smile.

"Oh, Miss Ana. I didn't know you were working here." Nate gestured to the stack of books she was tidying.

Her porcelain cheeks grew pink and she smiled. "First day on the job."

Pressing my lips together, I hid my own grin at how Nate had called her, "Miss Ana." Maybe sometimes he could be equally as cute as he was creepy.

"What can I do for you?" I asked the tall man.

His almost-black irises lit up. "Ah. I attended a production of *Emma* this afternoon and one of the audience members let me in on the secret that the nineties blockbuster film, *Clueless*, is in actuality based on Jane Austen's novel." He shook his head, amused—which for the record, looked a lot like murderous on Nate.

Suppressing a giggle at the visual of Nate watching *Clueless*, I nodded. "Yeah," I said, rounding the counter and heading over to the Jane Austen table. "Did you want a copy?" I grabbed one and handed it to him.

His lips twitched, and while I knew he was merely excited, it looked as if he was about to let his head fall back so he could let out a villainous cackle. Instead, he clutched the book to his black button-up.

"I've just finished *Pride and Prejudice*, so I was up for something else by her," he said, striding over to the checkout counter.

I can't say if it was how he was holding *Emma*, a story with a heroine who sees herself as an excellent matchmaker, or if it was how he'd called her "Miss Ana," but I was suddenly hit with an idea.

Glancing back at Ana, I saw her watching Nate with a kindness and grace her older brother had never possessed—or definitely had never shown Nate. The coffee shop owner's hair was unkempt, his clothes ill-fitting—they bunched in odd places and pulled in others on his thin, lanky frame—but under all of his worrisome word choice, the man had shown himself to be thoughtful, supportive, and even kinda funny as I'd gotten to know him better over the last year. Sure, he was still weird, and slightly off-putting, but Ana seemed like the sweet, spoonful of honey this bitter barista's cup needed.

Once he'd paid and headed out, Ana and I worked silently for a minute or two.

"You know, I never realized it growing up, but Nate's a really nice guy," I said, glancing up over the computer screen at my new employee.

Her cheeks turned a little redder this time. She wouldn't look at me. "He is. I'm so glad to hear he's doing well."

"He really is. The man's a genius behind the espresso machine."

Ana moved to a bookshelf, straightening books that were already very neat. "I'm not really into coffee," she said.

I bit my lip, wondering if that had been her subtle way of telling me she wasn't interested. "Tea then?" I asked, hopefully.

"Pepper." Ana smiled, looking over at me. "I see what you're doing. And while I do think Nate is a very nice guy, I'm really not looking for a relationship right now. I recently got out of something very serious in New York and... I need to focus on me for a while." Her eyes pleaded with me to understand.

"Of course," I said, hands up. "Sorry. I think I was under the influence of *Emma* there for a moment."

We both laughed and went back to work, but I watched Ana out of the corner of my eye. While she shared her brother's hair color and practically perfect cheekbones, she was a waif of a thing, barely reaching my shoulders. And at the mention of this relationship, she seemed to shrink into a shadow that could slip between bookshelves. I thought about what she'd said earlier about Juilliard, how she'd needed to get away. This relationship she'd mentioned must've had something to do with her decision, based on the pain I could read in her normally serene features.

"Plus," she said, pulling me out of my thoughts. "If this last week has taught me anything, it's that I need to focus on my family."

Messing with a stack of papers on the counter, I nodded to show my understanding. I don't know what I would do if anything happened to Maggie. Like my sister and me, Tommy and Ana had always been close.

Ana looked as if she was about to tip over. She set a small hand on a shelf to steady herself. "I can't believe I came so close to losing him." She shook her head.

I sighed, not sure what to say.

"I'm so glad they put that awful man behind bars so I don't have to worry about him coming back to finish the job." She shuddered.

Her mention of Duncan brought back my doubts. I know I had been convinced it was him at first, too. But I was beginning to doubt that more and more now that he was in custody. And if Jane Austen had taught me anything, it was that first impressions weren't always to be trusted. I also had to remember how I'd met him after hearing Karla label him "the scariest man ever." That had to have colored my first view of the man.

"Did you know him at all?" I asked, hoping to dig up anything that might give me a clearer picture.

Ana shook her head. "No, but Tommy hated him. Said he had a terrible temper and was always flying off the handle."

Narrowing my eyes, I prodded further. "What about Karla?" Just because the video clue was a dead-end, didn't mean there weren't other clues leading to Tommy's assistant.

At the mention of the woman, Ana rolled her eyes and made a spitting sound. "Pft. She'll stir up drama wherever she can. She smells weakness like you and I smell books," Ana continued, saying, "She pokes and stokes and creates problems wherever she goes."

I blinked, even though I'd suspected as much. "So why does your brother keep her around?"

Exhaling what sounded like years of arguments, Ana answered, "No one else can get his face to lose its shine like she can. And she's pretty good at shaping eyebrows, too."

It wasn't funny, but it had been a long few days and it all burst out of me in a loud laugh. Ana joined in. In moments, we were teary and holding our sides, apparently needing the release of emotion more than we both thought.

"Wow," I said, wiping my fingers under my eyes. "Well, I'm glad your brother's okay too."

Ana smiled over at me. "Thanks. He's not as bad as people think, you know?"

After the last few days, it surprised me that I honestly could say I did, or at least I was beginning to see it.

"I know."

"It just about killed me when I heard it could've been him with that knife in his back and then again when the police thought he could've been the one to kill Will." She shook her head. "Tommy would never hurt anyone. He's got the biggest heart."

I felt pretty strongly about how he'd hurt plenty of people—my sister included—but I also knew it was more likely attributed to his lack of awareness that other people existed outside of himself rather than the size of his heart. I nodded all the same, sure as Ana seemed that Tommy wasn't a murderer.

13

The next day, Liv and I took a long lunch to see a noon performance of *Sense and Sensibility* with my sister.

Though Maggie was getting her law degree and had always planned on joining our mother's practice, she had a love of theater which equaled my love of literature. And while she was taking a bit of a break from community theater while Hudson was little, my sister was still very much entrenched in the local acting community.

By the time we found her among the tents and treats of the festival, Maggie was wearing a Regency-style bonnet to keep the summer sun out of her face and was happily munching on a meat pie as she glanced at rings in an ornate jewelry booth.

"Already in character, I see." I eyed her pie and felt my stomach growl for lunch.

"K, I need one of these," Liv said, pointing to Maggie's headwear, "and one of these. Stat." Liv pointed at the pie.

Maggie laughed. "Sorry. I forgot to eat breakfast this morning and I was starving by the time I made it here."

Minutes later, Liv and I were biting into our own delicious, flaky pies and were decked out in our own bonnets. We headed over to the knoll where they were holding most of the performances. Maggie, being a mom, had a bag containing everything we could possibly need. She had a soft blanket for us to sit on, water and juice for us to drink, and even some trail mix in case we were still hungry.

We laughed and snacked and it felt good to let go a little after the last few tense days around Pine Crest.

Soon we lost ourselves in the Dashwood women's story, hating Willoughby when he broke Marianne's heart and swooning over Mr. Edward Ferrars. Tears streamed down our faces as Edward announced he was not the Mr. Ferrars who had gotten married, leaving him still very much able to propose to Elinor.

After the actors took their final bows and curtsies, Maggie pulled us up to the grassy "stage" to talk with some of the actors she knew.

"You were so great!" she said as she pulled Kathy, the woman who'd played Elinor Dashwood, into a tight hug.

Kathy beamed, stepping back to widen the circle as a few of her fellow players gathered around Maggie to say their hellos and collect their congratulations. I'd met Kathy a few times during past plays Maggie had been involved in. She put a hand on my shoulder and smiled a hello.

"How are you?" she asked.

I nodded. "Great. Glad the festival seems to be back on track."

Kathy and a few of the other ladies nodded and murmured regrets for Will.

Except Jenny, one of the other actresses, who let out a little squeak instead. She covered her mouth, eyes wide.

"Jenny, what is it?" Kathy asked, stepping closer. The rest of us leaned in.

"Did you not like Will?" I asked.

"Well, I don't know. Not me personally." Her voice was small and high like how I imagined a talking mouse might sound. She wrung her hands on her costume apron and glanced around nervously. "But I did hear something. You know how rumors are, though."

"Yeah, meant to be shared, and also ninety percent of every Jane Austen plot," the woman who'd played Mrs. Dashwood said with a husky chuckle. "Spill, dear."

Jenny lowered her already whispery voice to a volume just above a breath. "Well, I heard Will and Bonnie were splitting up." The other women gasped in disbelief. Jenny only nodded. "Apparently Will was having an affair and Bonnie found out."

"Really?" I asked, trying to keep the desperation I felt from making my tone too forceful.

Doubt shown clearly on all of the faces around me, all except the girl who'd played Marianne, whose lip curled slightly.

"Actually, it doesn't surprise me at all." She shook her head. "I was part of a few productions last year with Will and…" she paused, red blooming in patches on her face. "The man was pretty handsy. Always wanted to have private practice sessions with me. When I finally said yes to one, he ended up trying to kiss me."

Scoffing, I whispered, "What a creep. And right under Bonnie's nose, too?"

"Gross." Liv snorted and everyone nodded in agreement.

Will was turning out to be a much different person than I'd thought. Bonnie, too. The director had hidden everything so well. Seeing her and Will together, I would never have guessed they were having problems. A cold chill ran down my spine as I realized this gave Bonnie motive to kill Will. Adultery was right up there with money as the oldest motives for murder.

The actors began migrating back toward the costume tents. We waved our goodbyes and congratulated them once more.

When we were alone, Liv and Maggie leaned in close.

"Whoa." Liv shook her head. "Will sounds pretty awful."

"Yeah," I said. "Which makes me wonder if maybe the murder wasn't a case of mistaken identity after all."

When Maggie tipped her head in question, I explained.

"When I found the body, I'd thought it was Tommy. And the fact he was stabbed from behind made me wonder if the murderer had actually been trying to kill Tommy, but had mistakenly stabbed Will instead. Plus, I couldn't think of anyone who would want Will dead, and Tommy—well…" I shrugged.

Liv and Maggie nodded as we started back toward our blanket and stuff.

"Tommy is Tommy." Maggie wrinkled her nose, knowing full well the effect he had on most people.

"Right, but now we're learning Will wasn't so great either. Maybe I was wrong."

Liv blinked. "So who do you think did it if it was Will they meant to kill?"

I glanced around, making sure no one was within earshot. "Bonnie, for one. If her husband was having an affair, she had plenty of motive."

Chewing on her lip for a moment, Liv shook her head. "But people cheat on people all the time and they don't necessarily kill them."

Maggie nodded as she picked up the blanket we'd sat on

and folded it. "Right. Plus, they were working together still. I can't imagine her being okay with that if she was so mad at him."

I tried to share their optimism as I helped her pack up. "Or she could've been keeping him close until she could get her revenge."

Maggie frowned. "That's pretty creepy."

I agreed.

One thing was for certain, today had confirmed Miss Austen's lessons about people not always being who you thought they were. I'd been sure Will was well-liked in the community, only to find out he'd been hitting on women ten or more years his junior and having possible affairs behind his wife's back. It made a terrible feeling settle in my gut.

As we walked away from the stage, I glanced back one last time toward Tommy's trailer, the scene of the crime. I was fairly surprised to see someone exiting, but even more so to see it was Alex.

"Hey," I said to Maggie and Liv. "I see Alex over there, so I'll catch you two later."

They shared a wink and a giggle before waving goodbye. I ignored them and turned back toward the trailer.

Alex spotted me yards away and raised a hand in a wave. I did the same since we were still too far to hear each other.

"What a nice surprise," I said once we were closer, a big smile on my face.

He was in uniform and therefore sporting his normal serious-cop face, but he did return my smile and leaned down to kiss me. "It definitely is."

Hooking my arm through his, we walked along the edge of the festival grounds, letting the midday sun warm our faces.

"What were you doing at Tommy's trailer?" I asked. "Gathering evidence still?"

"Just asking Karla a few questions." He looked over at me, a smirk playing at the edge of his lips. "Someone gave us a tip she had motive for murder."

I laughed. "Sounds like a smart person."

"She is."

"But?" I asked pulling him to a stop.

His eyebrows furrowed. "There's no *but*. You're very smart, Pepper."

"No." I shook my head. "But your questions didn't lead anywhere?"

Alex glanced around us before answering. "No. Her alibi is sound. I knew before coming here today."

"So why question her?"

"For Duncan. I needed to see if she could shed any light on his story."

Rolling my eyes, I said, "Of course she's going to implicate the man. She was the one stirring up trouble between him and Tommy in the first place."

"Which she admitted to." Alex nodded. "You were right, she wanted to mess with them, Duncan especially. Apparently he had told Tommy to get a new assistant about a month ago and she overheard. She'd wanted to get him back, but hadn't meant for it to go this far."

I thought about when she'd come to see me the other day. She hadn't seemed remorseful in the least about Duncan's arrest. But who knew. Maybe she realized her mistake after. Or she was putting on a show for Alex.

He put a hand on my arm. "This really doesn't help Duncan, though," he said. "Especially since he's the only one besides Will who would have any cause to kill Tommy."

Squinting, I said, "Well, that may be up for debate. I

learned some interesting information after the play today." I took his arm again and we continued walking, skirting further and further around the tents and people until we were walking alone in the open park. Alex, sensing what I was doing, stayed quiet until then.

"Someone else mad at Tommy?" he asked finally.

I shook my head. "I think there's a possibility we were wrong about Tommy being the intended victim. What if Will was the mark all along?"

Alex chuckled. "Mark? Are we part of the mob now?"

Balling my fist, I gave him a light punch in the arm. "Don't make fun of me." But the smirk on my lips showed him I wasn't really upset. "I'm serious. Will was not the nice guy everyone thought he was. Apparently he was something of a sleaze, having affairs behind Bonnie's back."

"Did she know?"

"I heard she did, heard they were separating. I think you might want to look into Bonnie's alibi. I saw her near Tommy's trailer right before I found the body and she seemed weird, flustered."

"Adultery is a good motive," Alex ran his knuckles across his stubbled chin. "She seemed devastated when you guys found Will, though."

"Actors, all of them," I said, reminding him what we were dealing with. "The affair is only a rumor at this point, of course."

"Right." He stopped, pushing the toe of his shoe into the soft grass. "And you know what people say about rumors."

I squinted. "They're meant to be shared?" I said, quoting the woman who'd played Mrs. Dashwood.

Alex blinked. "They're usually so far from the truth you should never believe them."

"Oh." I laughed. "Yeah, that one… sure."

"Even so, I'll make sure to look into her." Alex's gaze met mine. "Thanks for the information." His eyes held a hint of an apology.

Even though we'd both apologized for our fight the other night, things still felt a little off. Us sharing information like this felt like the road back to normal.

He wrapped an arm around my shoulders, pulled me into a kiss, and then said, "Well, I gotta go. See you later?"

I nodded, waving as he left. I watched him walk away and reminded myself to write a thank you note to whatever genius designed the official Pine Crest police uniform pants.

Knowing Ana was watching the shop gave me a little wiggle room before I absolutely had to get back. And having been reminded by Alex about the validity of rumors—or lack thereof—I decided to see if I could get some answers about Duncan. That meant I needed to talk with Tommy.

So I turned back toward the festival and hoped he was at the trailer. But when I knocked on the door, Karla was the one who opened it with a whoosh.

"Hi!" I smiled up at her.

"Oh." Her face softened. "Sorry, I thought you were Tommy. He's supposed to meet me here to go over his lines, but still doesn't want to enter the 'crime scene.'" She rolled her eyes, using finger quotes around the last two words.

I didn't mention how it wasn't really appropriate to use quotes there as this actually had been a crime scene and quotes would imply he only thought it was. Instead, I put on my best "what a jerk" expression.

"What's up?" she asked, leaning up against the trailer handrail.

Before I could answer, Karla's attention moved to something behind me. I turned to see Tommy approaching.

"Finally!" she said.

Tommy flashed his assistant a grin I'm sure would be labeled a "devastating smile" in the scripts he received for his show. He winked at me jabbing a thumb toward Karla. "You see, Peppy? This girl can't get enough of me. Couldn't wait until I got here."

Karla and I shared a disgusted look. The guy was as dense as he was narcissistic. I suddenly wondered how much he would actually be able to tell me about Duncan. Would he know anything other than what Duncan did for him?

"TK, we've got work to do. Plus, you have dinner with your uncle tonight and he's having some problems with his knee again, so I thought it might be nice for you to get some takeout to bring to him."

As I watched Karla, I realized *she* was the person I should talk to about Duncan, not Tommy.

I bit my lip while I waited for them to work out the details.

Tommy turned his attention to me. "Did you need something from me, Peppy?"

"Uh... no. Karla, actually."

He clicked his tongue, then shimmied past her and into the trailer. Karla looked to me, expectantly.

Coming up with a quick plan, I said, "If you're not going to dinner with them tonight, you're welcome to come by and split that bottle of wine with me. I'm doing inventory the next few nights, so I'll be staying late at the shop and I would love the company."

Karla's eyes lit up at the mention. "I never turn down a good bottle of wine, or a chance to get out of dinner with Tommy's uncle. I can be there by eight."

14

I closed the shop at six that evening, sending Ana home despite her offer to help me with inventory.

"You've got dinner with your uncle and brother, right?"

She sighed, nodding. "They ask so many questions. 'What are you doing back home, Ana?' 'When are you going to start playing piano again?'"

"Sorry," I said. "But believe me, this is my very first time doing inventory and I know I'm going to be a terrible mess, so I'd rather not have any witnesses," I said, laughing.

"Okay, I'll see you tomorrow." She slung her purse over her shoulder and headed out.

I was surrounded by piles of books a few hours later when Karla knocked on the locked bookshop door. I smiled out of relief for the interruption and trotted over to let her in.

"Oh, thank goodness." I closed the door and locked it behind her. "I definitely need a wine break."

"Me too. Tonight was eyebrow night." She groaned. "I'll be honest, I definitely get less and less gentle the whinier he becomes." Karla plopped down on the couch in the back corner of the small shop and I brought over two tea mugs, a corkscrew, and the bottle.

"Sorry, it's either these or plastic cups."

Karla waved a hand. "The mugs are fine."

I opened the bottle and poured us each a small amount. While I'd gotten her here on the pretense of drinking wine, I didn't want to get her drunk. I wasn't some creep trying to drug information out of her. Plus, I got the impression Karla was someone whose secrets sat in her mind about as long as a new J.K. Rowling book stayed on a bookstore shelf.

For the first half hour, we simply shared stories about her boss, and I asked if she knew any other stars in Hollywood. She named a few I'd heard of, but I was clueless about most of the others she talked about, preferring a good book to most television. We were talking so much that neither of us did much drinking, and I was just sipping the last of my half glass by the time a break in conversation came.

Now was my chance. I set down my mug.

"So you really think Duncan did this?"

Karla shrugged. "All the evidence is there."

"Is it?"

"The knife, their fight, Duncan's temper." She touched a new finger as she listed each thing. "You thought it was TK when you found the body. It makes sense the killer would've, too."

I chewed on my lip for a moment, thinking. "Are you sure he asked you to buy him a knife?"

She nodded.

"What were his exact words?" I asked.

"He said, 'Get me everything I'll need to do some fishing.'"

A glimmer of hope formed in my mind. "But he's from

the city like you. Remember how you didn't know a fisherman would use a knife. He wouldn't have known either."

She frowned, pouring herself more wine. "Well…"

"How'd you decide what to buy him?"

"I looked it up." Her shoulders slumped forward a bit. "But just because he didn't ask me specifically to buy the knife doesn't mean he didn't use it. Duncan must've seen the knife sitting there the night before when he was fighting with TK." She sat up.

"What was the fight about?"

This made her curl her fingers around her mug of wine. "I may have started it, actually. Don't worry, I told the police already."

"You wanted to get back at Duncan for telling Tommy to fire you?" I leaned forward.

Karla shook her head, immediately. "No. I mean, that sucked, don't get me wrong. But I already knew the guy wouldn't fire me. He's way too worried about his eyebrows to ever let me go without a fight." Her cheeks reddened a little and she took a long sip. "It was something else."

I waited.

Finally, she met my gaze and said, "I asked Duncan to put a good word in with a director friend of his for a part on a show I wanted. He refused, saying it wasn't ethical, but I know he's done stuff like that before."

Oh. This was making more sense. "So you tried to get rid of him."

She nodded.

"By framing him for murder?"

Her nod screeched to a halt and turned into a defiant shake. "I didn't know they would actually arrest him. I had no idea there was more evidence against the guy than what I was telling the police."

"So the fight wasn't as bad as you made it sound?"

Karla's eyes widened. "No. That was really bad. Duncan got super mad. His face was all red and he was pacing all over the trailer. I wasn't exaggerating when I told you he has a really bad temper."

I sighed. Hmm… That didn't help me much.

In my silence, Karla went on. "But I will admit he hasn't always been like this. It's mostly the last few months he's been so mean."

I thought back to when he had dinner with us and how he'd mentioned the stress he'd been under lately. Thinking of the dinner reminded me of my mother, of how happy she'd looked when she was talking to Duncan. I decided to strike out on a whim.

"Karla, do you really think Duncan killed Will?"

She shook her head.

"Then you have to tell the police."

Karla sipped on her wine for a few moments. "I know. You don't think they'll tell Thomas about all of this, do you?" She looked across the coffee table at me.

"About what?"

She lifted one shoulder. "That I tried to get Duncan in trouble."

I pulled in a slow breath. "I can't see any reason they would. Why do you care?" I asked, narrowing my eyes at her.

Karla took a drink. "No reason." But when I stared her down, she said, "I like him, okay?"

"Duncan?" Talk about May/December.

"No!" Karla giggled. "TK. I know I complain about him, but it's mostly my way of hiding my true feelings. He's an amazing actor, and I don't know, we spend almost every day together. He's not bossy *all* the time."

I wondered if my eyes got all dreamy like that when I talked about Alex. Just thinking of him made my stomach flutter excitedly. The realization made me soften a little to Karla.

She continued talking, her face tightening out of the dewy, lovestruck version of a moment ago. "But now that *she's* around, you'd think I was invisible."

Blinking, I asked, "She?"

"Ana." Karla snapped the name out like a swear word.

"His sister?"

"Yeah. He drops everything for her at a moment's notice. The second she's in trouble, he's by her side."

Ana? Trouble? I almost laughed out loud. The girl was so sweet and innocent, I doubted her parents had needed to scold her once during her entire childhood. But then I remembered Karla complaining about her yesterday. What had she said? Something about her throwing away all of the money Tommy spent on her fancy school. I focused on Karla who wrinkled her nose in disgust.

"He's always talking about how close they are, but he had to find out from someone else how she'd flunked out of Juilliard and ran home." Karla cocked an eyebrow at me.

My mind reeled. "Flunked? I thought she was taking a break after graduation."

Karla laughed. "It's hard to take a break after graduation when you didn't even graduate."

Thinking back to my talk with Ana earlier, I went out on a limb. "Did her dropping out have to do with the relationship she was in?"

Touching the tip of her nose with her pointer finger, Karla winked at me. "I can't decide if her grades were worse when she and mystery guy were together, and she 'didn't have time' for her classes, or when he left her and she 'didn't have the energy.'" Karla's face was pulled into a frown, but her concern was an obvious mask. The woman seemed to thrive on telling secrets. "It's why TK came back here in the first place. Playing Darcy in the festival was simply a ruse Duncan thought up so the gossip columns might not find out why he was really here."

I blinked. "Did he ever find out what happened to make her leave?"

She shrugged. "Her boyfriend broke up with her, so I just guessed that was it. She got too sad and needed to come home. He was going to ask Ana more about what happened, tonight."

Ana *had* said she wasn't looking forward to dinner because of all of the questions. It looked like tonight wasn't going to be any better for her.

Karla tipped her cup back and swallowed the last bit of her wine. "I've got to get back."

"Sure," I said, but my voice felt like it wasn't mine, like it was far away. My mind was too focused on Ana. I did manage enough wherewithal to walk Karla to the door and unlock it. Opening the door, I stepped aside so she could leave.

She paused outside the door, looking back. "Thanks for the break and for the conversation." And with that, she was gone, walking toward the park as the sun dipped behind the mountains in the distance.

Sighing, I closed the door and locked it. Questions about what Karla said crowded my thoughts like a slow fog, rolling in until it enveloped everything. I went over to the computer and looked up Ana's name and Juilliard. Karla had been right. I couldn't find her name included in any of the recent graduation lists. Other than that, I couldn't find anything else about Ana or her mystery guy. Too bad the internet wasn't as thorough as the Pine Crest gossip circuit. After a few more minutes of fruitless searching, the stack of books next to me began calling, and I returned to my inventory work.

Liv sent me a picture a little while later of Hammy on her evening walk. I hadn't brought her to work with me today because of the play, not wanting to risk her barking or making a scene during the performance. I knew Liv was taking good care of her, but I missed her company. Running my hands up and down my arms, I realized my skin was raised into goosebumps, even though I wasn't the least bit cold. Ignoring the odd feeling, I lost myself in my work.

I finally gave up for the night around eleven, swiping my purse from under the counter and stifling a yawn. It was pitch-black outside. I blearily stumbled out of the door, and then fumbled with the old lock until it finally clicked into place. When I turned around, however, I had to hop to avoid stepping on something sitting on the shop doorstep. All feelings of fatigue left me as I stared down at the object.

It was a hardback book, which wasn't all that surprising to see in front of a bookshop. What had my blood running cold was the knife stabbed into the cover.

My heart beat so fast it made my head feel light and wobbly. I backed up a few feet, almost falling off the edge of the sidewalk. A knife stabbed into a book. So soon after a knife stabbed into a back. This was a warning. I needed to call Alex. I slipped my phone from my purse and was about to call him when I heard a rustling behind me.

Whirling around, I eyed the mouth of the alley next to my building. My neighbor was a dentist's office and they rarely stayed late, never past six. Was the book a warning or had it been meant as a distraction? Could the stabber still be close by? My feet felt frozen in one spot, until I heard something scrape across the concrete mere feet away. I glanced at the bookshop. There was no way I was going to get that darn, old door unlocked quickly.

So I ran.

My lungs burned as I pulled in frantic breath after frantic breath. I couldn't tell if the pounding footsteps were only mine or if the scraping, rustling, book-stabbing someone was following me to finish the job. After a few hundred feet, I realized I'd run in the direction of the park where there were no streetlights. My eyes began to adjust to the lack of light. Eerie tendrils of fog crept over the grass, reaching out onto the deserted streets in front of me. It was then I noticed I was still clutching my phone in my palm. Right. Alex. I dialed his number, trying not to let the effort slow my steps.

"Hey," Alex said, answering right away.

"Someone left a knife stabbed into a book outside," I panted out each word. "I think they were still there." My side was beginning to ache. I slowed slightly.

Alex's slightly sleepy voice turned tense. "Where?"

I glanced over my shoulder, squinting at the sidewalks and empty streets. "By the shop, I—" A shiver ran up my spine as I thought I saw something.

When I turned back around to look where I was running. I tripped on an uneven section of the sidewalk, my ankle buckling beneath me with a pain that made me cry out. Then I was airborne, moving sideways in a flight plan labeled *disaster*. My phone flew from my grasp, landing feet away from me with a crack. My hip and wrist bounced off the concrete and then I settled with a sickening slide.

Writhing on the concrete in hot, pulsing pain for a few seconds, I finally sat up. My body hurt like the dickens, though. I tried to push myself up so I could stand, but my wrist and my ankle simultaneously screamed out very convincing arguments to stay down. I held my ankle with my good hand for a minute, then slithered on the ground toward my phone. It was completely cracked, the screen refused to turn on.

It was then I heard the footsteps approaching. Fast.

15

There was no way Alex could've gotten here so soon. Right? It had to be the stabber.

I closed my eyes, unable to watch. But then I realized, if I was a goner anyway, I might as well figure out who did it before I died. Peeling open one eye at a time, I watched the figure approach from down the street.

I rummaged through my purse for any sort of weapon, but only found some breath spray and keys. They would have to do. I stuck my keys in between my fingers like tiny Wolverine claws, and then held up the spray thinking I might be able to blind them for a minute or two. Stabbing seemed like an activity that relied on a fair amount of visual precision.

A tall shape appeared out of the fog, and my breath caught in my throat.

"Pepper?" Alex's voice was like a shot of morphine, instant relief.

Suppressing a relieved sob, I cried out, "Alex!" My fingers relaxed and the keys fell from between them, settling in my lap.

Alex closed the distance between us as if he were an Olympic sprinter. He skidded to a stop by my side. "Are you hurt? Did someone do this to you?"

"Yes—er—no." I shook my head then nodded it. "I am hurt, but it's because I tripped and fell." My wrist must've picked up a gnarly scrape from the concrete based on how it was stinging, and I bet I was going to have a whopper of a bruise on my hip, but the worst pain was my foot. I reached down to grab my ankle and I felt hot tears slide down my cheeks, whether from relief or pain, I couldn't quite tell.

"You didn't hit your head, did you?" he asked.

"No, my ankle."

Alex followed my attention and tried to look at my foot, but it was too dark to tell anything much. He leaned forward, swiping a tear from my cheek. Before I knew what was happening, he had wrapped his arms around me and scooped me up, carrying me back toward the shop. It was like when Colonel Brandon carried Marianne when she went out dur—

"Wait. Wait. My phone," I said, reaching back toward the broken thing. The screen may be broken, but maybe I could save the data.

Complying, Alex went back and we located the shattered remains. I snuggled in close to the space under his chin, phone in hand. So maybe not *exactly* like Marianne.

As he carried me, I realized he wasn't in uniform. My fingers gripped the soft cotton of a T-shirt instead of the stiff fabric of his uniform.

"How'd you find me so fast?"

"I was just getting off my shift for the night and on my way home when you called."

We approached the lights of the bookshop as Frank pulled up in his cruiser, parking it next to Alex's truck. Frank was still in uniform, but the top few buttons of his shirt were undone, and he looked equally as tired as Alex. Rushing over to us, he asked, "She okay?"

Alex nodded. "Probably only a sprain."

"I heard something in the alley and I got scared," I added.

Frank said, "Everyone's on edge since Will's murder. But Pepper, you don't need to worry so much. You know we've got Duncan in custody." He peered at me, pity lacing his words.

I scoffed from where I hung in Alex's arms. "Um, pretty sure you've got the wrong guy behind bars, there Frank-o." I laced my own words with a hint of the frustration I felt. Who was Frank to treat me like I was being silly and overreactive?

He shrugged. "Still, I really don't think anyone's hiding outside the bookstore trying to hurt you." He glanced down the alley. "You likely heard a rat, or Martin."

Martin was Pine Crest's most infamous street cat. He was as big as a springer spaniel, orange, and older than me —or so it seemed. Anytime something inexplicable happened, it was routinely blamed on the frisky, old feline. It didn't hurt that he was often spotted nearby any sort of calamity.

Rolling my eyes, I said, "I didn't realize Martin had grown opposable thumbs and enough strength to stab a knife through a book."

Frank's forehead wrinkled. "What?"

"I didn't only hear noises. Seeing *that* when I left tonight ramped things up a bit." I pointed at the doorstep of the bookshop.

Frank looked, but the creases in his face only deepened. I followed his gaze.

"Uh, Peps," Alex said.

I blinked as I looked at the door. The book, the knife, all of it was literally… gone.

"The doormat?" Frank mumbled the question.

Pointing with the arm not clutching Alex, I said, "What? It was right there." Wild eyed, I looked to Frank. "The killer was in the alley. When I ran away they must've taken it back."

Frank wouldn't meet my gaze. He rubbed the back of his neck. "I—I'll check the perimeter of the building." He shuffled away, but I didn't miss the look he gave Alex before disappearing around the corner, large flashlight in hand.

It was a clear, *Man, your girlfriend's lost it*, look if I'd ever seen one.

"I haven't lost it, Frank!" I yelled after him—admittedly, not helping my case one bit. I leaned back a little so I could see Alex's face. "You believe me, right?"

Alex swallowed, dipping his head slowly. "Mi pimienta, I—"

"Oh no. Don't you cute-Spanish-nickname me right now. You *don't* believe me?" I wiggled in his arms. "I want to get down."

"Your ankle is—"

I continued to squirm. "I'd rather rough it on one leg than let someone who doesn't believe me carry me around."

He lowered me to the ground carefully. I didn't even try to put any weight on my right foot, knowing from the sharp and throbbing pain radiating through that it was at least sprained. Even though I was on the ground now, Alex kept his arms wrapped around my waist, holding me tight. Immediately missing being in his arms, I sank forward, pressing my face into his chest.

"I can't believe you think I'm crazy, too," I said, my words muffled by his shirt. I looked up at his chin.

He tucked it and peered down at me. "I think you've been here late, by yourself, and you've been looking at way too many books for inventory. Be honest. Isn't it a slight possibility you imagined it?"

I closed my eyes. *Was it?* I tried to picture the knife, the book, any detail. "It was a kitchen knife, a six-inch blade—I'm guessing—with a black handle. The book was hardbound, the old cloth kind with gold lettering. Like the copy of *Persuasion* I was reading the other day when we went hiking." I paused, frowning as my hand patted my purse.

Unzipping the top, I rummaged through the veritable black hole that was my old school bag, now purse. I normally carried a few books—along with half my apartment, apparently—with me, just in case. But tonight all I could find was the copy of *Walden* I'd recently started. I knew I'd had *Persuasion* in my purse, too, remembering placing it there this morning. But it wasn't there.

Alex watched, eyebrows furrowed.

My head snapped up. "It's not here. It was *my* book they stabbed." That made the fear all the more real. "They got into my purse?"

Seeming to take this somewhat seriously now, Alex asked, "Did you leave the book lying out anywhere?"

I closed my eyes and thought. Snapping them open, I nodded. "Not *out*, but at the play today. Maggie, Liv, and I left our stuff for a few minutes when we went to talk with the actors." Just as suddenly as the realization hit me, hopelessness followed. "Pretty much anyone walking by could've taken it, though. I wasn't watching."

Alex eyed me.

"What? I had my wallet in my pocket. Plus, it's Pine Crest. Most people don't even lock their doors."

He shook his head.

"Not *me*, but a lot of people."

"So anyone could've gotten into your bag during that time and taken it." He arched an eyebrow. "And you didn't notice it was lighter?"

Pressing my lips forward for a second, I admitted, "I think I *did* notice, but I thought I was getting stronger from having to lift all of the boxes and stacks of books in the store."

Alex chuckled.

I saw Frank's flashlight beam bounce around the far side of the building.

"So you believe me now?" I asked, hoping the pleading tone was all in my head.

He sighed. Then nodded.

"And this is yet another piece of evidence in favor of Duncan, right?"

He nodded again. "Correct."

Frank appeared and clicked his flashlight off as he approached us. "Nothing, Pepper. Your doors are all locked and haven't been tampered with. I think you're okay."

Alex held out his hand and Frank shook it. "Thanks for coming. I've got her from here."

Frank winked at me and walked to the cruiser, finally headed home. He, like Alex, was unmarried and had no kids, so I knew it wasn't too much of an inconvenience that he had stopped. His large tabby cat, Karl, might be slightly upset by his late arrival, but other than that, Frank might just need an extra shot in his coffee tomorrow. I knew he and Alex were putting in long days trying to catch this killer, and as much as I was annoyed he hadn't believed me, I appreciated him stopping.

We watched him pull away. Alex looked at me. "Gonna let me carry you to the truck, or do I have to watch you hop over there?" His mouth quirked up at one end.

Why did he look so sexy when he was teasing me? I glared at him, but hooked my arms around his neck, as he bent to pick me up again. He kissed my cheek as he did so, making me glad he was holding me since I was sure my knees would've been mush after such a display.

After depositing me gently into the passenger seat of his truck, Alex checked the locks on the bookshop one last time. Then he drove me home. It took a second of maneuvering, but he got me out and I kicked the passenger door shut with my good foot. He carried me as far as the apartment. There, I fiddled with my keys and then the lock until he stumbled inside with me still in his arms.

Liv and Carson looked up from where they sat on the floor, cards in between them and Hammy sacked out in her bed close by. The dog snorted and rolled up, as the door closed behind us. She scrambled past Liv and Carson then danced around Alex's feet, jumping up and attempting to reach me. I dropped my hand down and she licked it twice, then I looked back to Liv.

My best friend's eyes went wide and her mouth curved into a surprised smile as she took us in. "Oh. My. Gosh. Did the two of you elope or something?"

Alex and I both sputtered incoherent syllables, and I could see the heat in my cheeks mirrored in the blush creeping into Alex's.

"What?" I asked, finally.

Liv pointed at us. "You look like you're carrying her over the threshold, man."

Carson shook his head and threw down his cards. "Alex, I've talked to you about this before. You can't *do* stuff like this. Makes the rest of us guys look bad." His frustrated gaze turned on Liv and his head bobbed a bit as if he were trying to figure out the logistics of picking up his own girlfriend.

"Pepper's hurt." Alex had no time for Liv's wedding fantasy—misplaced as it was. He strode forward and nudged open my bedroom door. Then he set me on my bed.

The heat in my cheeks from Liv's misunderstanding only increased when I saw the state of my room. Clothes were draped over my desk, chair, and the corner of my mattress. I hoped none of them were underwear. Hammy jumped up on the bed, immediately attacking my face with her prescribed treatment, licking. I laughed and pushed her to the side until she settled next to me.

Racing into the doorway, Liv asked, "Hurt? What happened?"

"I'll tell you while we grab something to ice her ankle," Alex said, disappearing into the kitchen, Liv on his heels.

16

Alex must've given Liv the quick and dirty version of what had transpired that night, because by the time they came back moments later, concern marred her normally pristine features and she was spinning her thumb ring like she did whenever she was worried.

"Let me get some extra pillows," she said, darting out into the living room.

Alex nodded, easing my foot out of the black flat I was wearing. Then he tugged my legging up so it was up on my calf. He'd located a bag of frozen peas which had to be at least a year old—both Liv and I hated peas.

Grabbing a T-shirt from the edge of the bed, he raised his eyebrows in question. I nodded and he wrapped the bag of frozen veggies in the shirt and then placed it gently around my swollen ankle. The relief was immediate. I closed my eyes and lay back.

"Pillows!" Liv sang as she galloped into the room with every throw pillow from our couch. She helped Alex position them under my knee and foot so the whole cold contraption was lifted up. Carson watched from the doorway.

Alex sighed, finally seeming to relax now that I was in bed and comfortable. He pulled out the chair from my desk, ignoring the clothes draped on the back—even though they had to be killing a neat freak like him—and sat next to my side.

I reached my hand out toward him, laughing slightly. "You are *not* going to sit there all night." I let my head move back-and-forth in a firm no. "You are dead tired and need to get a good night's sleep. Liv will take care of me from here."

Indecision was nowhere to be found in Alex's tone as he said, "I'm not leaving you after what happened tonight." Even without his uniform, he sounded like a cop giving orders.

Relief washed over me, and I realized I hadn't actually wanted him to go.

Alex stood. "But I haven't had dinner yet. You have anything to eat other than Pop-Tarts and bagels?"

I glared at him.

"I just stocked the fridge with sandwich makings," Carson said from the doorway. He tipped his head to the side. "Come on, I could go for one, too. Girls?"

After Liv and I declined, the two of them headed into the kitchen. Using the chair Alex had already pulled next to my bed, Liv plopped down. "How you feeling?" She scanned me as if checking for any other wounds.

I groaned as I repositioned myself, my battered hip pulsing with a deep pain. "Anymore veggies we're never gonna eat hanging out in the freezer?" I patted my side. "Landed pretty hard on the old saddle bag."

Liv grabbed my hand, pulling it toward her and

swiveling it so she could see the long scrape running the length of my hand and part of my forearm. "This'll need attention as well." She got up and padded out of my room, returning with more bags of frozen food, some Ibuprofen for the pain, and our emergency kit. She dressed the scrape silently while I took a swig of water to down the painkiller and then smooshed the bag of broccoli onto my side, sighing in relief.

Once I had a clean bandage wrapped around my wrist, Liv leaned back, her brown eyes meeting mine. "This is getting pretty scary, Peps."

"Yeah," I said through a grimace. "But it also means I must be on to something if they're desperate enough to threaten me."

"Alex said it was your book."

I nodded. "At least I think it is."

"And Duncan's in custody, so it couldn't have been him. Who do you think did it?"

Her question made my nose wrinkle in frustration. "That's the thing. I can't figure it out. I must know something important enough to make the killer come after me, I just can't figure out what." I tapped my fingers against the cold plastic of the broccoli bag. "Karla is out, I think. She's kinda in love with Tommy, and even though she started a bunch of drama and is mad at how close he is with Ana, I don't think she would hurt him." I paused. "Plus she had left my shop only hours before. If she really wanted to hurt me, she could've done it when it was the two of us."

Liv shook her head. "So Duncan's out, Karla's out. Anyone else who knew you were going to be at the shop late tonight?"

I thought about it. "Tommy might've overheard me

asking Karla, but he and Ana were having dinner with their uncle."

Liv's eyebrows rose. "Most dinners I've been to don't last until eleven."

I pressed my lips together as I thought. Tommy was an actor. He could very well be pretending to be innocent in this whole mess. "I guess," I said, not wanting to think about this anymore. Grimacing as I tried to move my foot, I leaned back into my pillow.

Just then, Alex walked back into the room with an already half-eaten sandwich in one hand. He took another big bite as he sat on the other side of my bed.

I yawned. "Well, we're not going to figure anything out tonight. It's past midnight. You should get some sleep, Liv."

Liv watched me.

"I'll be fine!" I laughed. "Hammy the protector will keep me safe." I glanced at the small dog, curled up by my other foot, snoring loudly. "And I've got this guy as backup if she fails," I said, reaching over and patting Alex's chest as he ate the last bite of his short-lived sandwich, saluting in answer since his mouth was full.

Finally letting her worried face relax, Liv sighed. "Okay, I'll be in my room. Yell if you need anything."

I blew her a kiss and she did the same before shutting the door behind her.

"How're you feeling?" Alex asked, reaching forward to adjust the frozen peas on my ankle.

"Like today chewed me up and spit me out." I chuckled. "But I'll be okay." I scooted a little closer to him, as he sat back.

Careful not to disturb Hammy with his long legs, Alex reclined, leaning into my headboard. A long tired sigh lifted his chest. He wrapped an arm around my shoulder, pulling me close. We sat there in a cozy silence for a few moments, and I began to forget about the pulsing pain radiating through my ankle and hip. Fatigue settled over me, and I wrapped my arms around him, laying my head on his chest as I closed my eyes.

Alex's steady pulse and measured breathing made any remaining tenseness in my body slip away. I breathed in his laundry-soap-and-peppermint-gum scent, wishing I could bottle it like cologne. He kissed the top of my head, hugging me even closer.

Within minutes, Hamburger's snores weren't the only ones filling my small bedroom.

I WOKE WITH A START, the ghost of the stabbed book warning sitting ominously in the back of my mind.

Blinking, I glanced at the clock. It was three o'clock in the morning. Alex's arms were still wrapped tightly around me, but Hammy had moved, managing to wedge herself in between the two of us.

And despite the scare I'd received just hours earlier, I couldn't help but smile. I was wrapped up, safe. Everything was okay. I reached over to click off my bedside lamp and then snuggled back into Alex's chest, drifting back to sleep.

I woke hours later to the sunlight streaming in through my window. Hammy and Alex were gone, the only evidence of their presence being the rumpled spots on the duvet, they'd left behind. I sat up, reaching forward to check my ankle. The vegetables were officially warm. I moved the squishy bags onto the chair next to my bed as I tried to circle my foot.

Pain still zinged through it, but it was decidedly better

than it had been last night. Either that or the ache in my hip and wrist had grown, making my ankle *seem* like it hurt less. Laying there for a few moments, I started to feel antsy, like I'm sure Jane Bennet felt when she was stuck, sick at Netherfield Park for all of those days. At the thought of *days* stuck in bed, I sat up. That was *not* going to be me.

Testing my foot carefully, hand on the back of the chair to steady myself, I lifted myself off the bed and tried putting a little weight on the leg.

"Ouch, ouch, ouch," I murmured, pulling the foot up. Nope. Still not up to walking on it.

I used the wall and my furniture to make my way out of my bedroom and into the living room. Alex looked up from where he sat at our small kitchen table, a paperback bent in half in his hands and Hammy curled up in his lap. He was freshly showered and already in his uniform. A pair of crutches were leaning against the kitchen counter. I smiled, hopping forward.

His eyes lit up when they saw me, but his attention quickly moved to the foot I was holding up off the floor. "Morning. How's it feeling?"

"Better?" I said, tipping my head to the side. "Still can't put my weight on it, but it happened so late last night I can't tell if it's had enough time." I looked around the apartment. "Liv gone?"

He nodded. "After I got back from running home to shower and grab you those," he pointed to the crutches, "I convinced her we would be fine and she should head into work for a bit." Alex closed his book, moved the dog off him, and made his way over to me, kneeling down to examine my ankle. "It's still pretty swollen." He shook his head. "You want me to take you to the hospital?"

I sighed. The Pine Crest Memorial Hospital was chock

full of my parents' friends and a growing number of my old classmates. I knew the story of my fall would get around town regardless—I was going to attract some attention using these crutches—but if I could avoid the heart of the lions' den, it would be something.

"I'd rather wait a few days and see if the pain goes away," I said, letting go of the wall to show him how good I was, but I wobbled slightly.

"Think you'll be able to manage a stop at the festival?"

My ears perked up like Hammy's did whenever she heard the word *walk*. "Festival?"

Alex nodded. "I want to talk to people about Bonnie's alibi. Maybe one of the actors saw someone getting into your purse, too."

"And I get to come along?" I asked, once the metal contraptions were crammed under each of my arms, already pinching me uncomfortably.

He smirked. "Well, I'm not leaving you by yourself with this stabber on the loose. Plus, you're going to look pretty pathetic in those crutches, maybe we can drum up some sympathy."

"Happy to help." I laughed.

Alex took care of walking Hammy while I got myself ready. Honestly, with how long it took, they probably could've walked around the whole of Pine Crest, twice. But finally, I was washed and dressed and ready to go.

I checked my watch as I fumbled my way into the truck. "Oh! The shop!" It was ten minutes until I was supposed to open and I'd almost completely forgotten.

"Pepper, I don't feel okay with you being there by yourself…" Alex started the engine, but shook his head.

"No, it's okay. Ana's coming in for the opening shift,

today. I'll just need to unlock the shop for her and then she can watch the place while we go question people."

I definitely wasn't going to miss out on Alex letting me tag along during an investigation.

"You stay here," I told him once he pulled up to the shop, knowing I'd be faster alone.

Ana was waiting outside the front door when we parked, her cell phone in hand.

"Oh, thank goodness. I called you a bunch. I thought something had…" she petered out as she watched me clatter over on my crutches. "Okay, something *did* happen. Is everything okay?"

"Long story. One which involves my phone meeting a clumsy and cracked end." I shook my head. "All of which I'll be happy to tell you this afternoon, but right now we have a few things to do." I met her eyes, wondering how boss-like it was to have to plead with your only employee. "Do you mind running things on your own again this morning? I shouldn't be more than a few hours."

"Of course." Ana assured me as I unlocked the door for her.

"Here," I said, handing her my spare key. "Just in case something like this happens again."

Ana clicked the key onto her ring with her others and nodded, following me inside so I could turn on the computer system for her. I hobbled back to the truck minutes later after promising Ana I'd be back soon.

With that done, Alex and I made it to the festival as it opened. It took me the walk from the parking lot to figure out how to use those darn crutches in the grass, but I think it probably helped me look even more pathetic. The problem was, they also made me super sweaty. Which meant half the time Alex was questioning the actors, I was a few feet away, panting and wiping sweat off my forehead.

He flipped his notebook closed as he said thank you to a pair in Regency dress and turned toward me.

"I think I need to wrap these rubber bits in towels," I said, pulling the crutches out from under each sweaty pit. "Things are getting slippery under here."

Alex smiled, but he was already checking the crowd for anyone else he could talk with.

"Any luck so far?" I asked.

He shook his head. "I can't get a single person to pin Bonnie down the morning of the murder. Everyone says she was 'bouncing about' and 'here and there' which is probably the least helpful thing I could hear right now." He sighed. "And no one remembers seeing anyone rifling through a purse like yours the day of the *Sense and Sensibility* performance."

Behind Alex, I saw Sarah, Bonnie's assistant, meeting with a few of the actors. I noticed her attention slip from them to us, namely to Alex. She kept talking, but her eyes continually flicked over to us.

Stumbling forward in a mess of metal and limbs, I scooted closer to Alex, whispering, "Don't look, but at your six there's a blonde, twenty-something, her name is Sarah. She's Bonnie's assistant. By the way she keeps looking at you, I'd say she knows something."

Alex nodded, flipping his notepad back open before pivoting and striding over to her. I hobbled along behind him, arriving as he motioned to my bag.

"…this bag sitting out unattended on a blue-plaid blanket right after the show?"

Sarah glanced at my bag, then shook her head almost

violently. She swallowed and pulled in a deep breath. "I'm sorry. I didn't. After the show is always a bit of a whirlwind."

I felt myself slump forward on the crutches. Gosh, this questioning people thing was disheartening, and boring. Alex, the true professional, didn't let any such fatigue show in his posture or on his face, even if I was pretty sure he felt the same as I did.

Sarah's eyes flitted about, looking between us and then at the festival crowds as if she was searching for someone.

I was about to leave her, sure she was just stressing over the upcoming performance this afternoon, when she blurted out, "Can I talk to you… two? In here?" She motioned to Bonnie's director tent behind her.

Alex and I glanced at each other for a split second. Then we nodded and followed her inside.

17

The tent offered a slight reprieve from the hot sun. The scent of warm grass consumed the small space and though it was only a few degrees cooler than outside, simply being out of the direct sunlight felt amazing. I blinked as my eyes adjusted, smiling as I saw two chairs sitting across from a desk to my right.

I think I laughed out loud with relief as I tottered over and sank into the closest one. "Oh, how I love you, chair." I closed my eyes for a quick second and let the cursed crutches clatter to the ground next to me. I held my arms up slightly to air out my sweaty pits.

Alex snorted, knelt down to pick up after me, and leaned the crutches against the desk before taking a seat next to me. Sarah settled behind the desk, fingers tapping on the desk that was piled high with scripts and books.

"So what can we do for you?" Alex asked, shooting her his impossible-to-read, police officer expression.

Sarah looked like she was about to throw up. Her face was pale and yet her neck was flushed with color. She winced as if some invisible someone was punching her in the gut. Finally, she opened her mouth.

"It's my fault!" she blurted out, eyes wild. She watched the fabric flap which made up the door to the tent as if someone might come bursting through at any moment.

My spine straightened. I felt like jumping up, cheering, screaming, and also running away. *Her?*

I blinked, sitting forward instead of acting on my other impulses, knowing those other reactions probably didn't fit in with Alex's calm, don't show them what you're thinking strategy.

Alex took a measured breath. "Sorry?"

"I'm the reason Will's dead. I was sleeping with him behind Bonnie's back." Her words broke, crumbled into sobs. "I'm sorry I didn't say anything sooner. I was worried about what people would think, but I haven't been able to grieve openly and now Bonnie's put me in charge so she can set up the funeral even though *I'm* the one who really needs the time off."

The suspense loosened its grip on my heart and I sat back, breathing for the first time since she'd yelled out her confession. We were talking adultery, not murder.

"And how long had this been going on?" Alex asked, jotting something down in his notebook.

"Just a few months, but—" she gulped back a sob, "—we were in love. The murderer has to be Bonnie. She caught us a few weeks back."

Alex furrowed his eyebrows. "And how did she react?"

Sarah took a shuddery breath, blinking. "Well, actually, she was—really calm." The young woman sniffed, breathing a little more slowly. "But that's weird. Right? She told me I could have him, she was filing for divorce."

So they really *were* separated, then. I picked at my thumbnail as I thought.

"I know it's her! It has to be." Sarah looked down at the desk, losing a bit of her steam.

"Did Will seem to think she was a threat?" Alex asked.

Sarah shook her head.

We all took a long inhale. That didn't mean anything definitive, but it also didn't help us pin anything on Bonnie. There was a stack of playbills for *Pride and Prejudice* sitting on the corner of the desk nearest to me, and in my need to do something, I reached out and grabbed one, flipping through it.

Sarah noticed and said, "Those are the old ones. We had to have a new set printed after Thomas King decided to *grace* us with his presence." She rolled her eyes.

I flipped past the sponsors and the list of acts, stopping at Bonnie's director bio.

This is the sixth play Bonnie Kemper has had the pleasure of directing. After growing up as a child performer in the Pine Crest Players, participating in over fifty productions from the age of seven on, she's proud to take Burt Phillip's place as head director. She loves to cook and is always looking for a new recipe to try out.

Huh. Well that didn't help.

"Did Bonnie say anything to you about Thomas King showing up? Was she mad about the change?" Alex asked.

Oh, so he was going for that line of questioning. I raised my eyebrows, but kept my eyes on the program as I listened to Sarah's response.

"She was stressed. We all were. But I think only Will was really all that mad. Here he'd worked so hard to prepare and Tommy waltzes in and takes the starring role." She must've seen her words pique a slight interest in Alex, because she added, "To be fair, even Ana was frustrated with Tommy showing up out of the blue."

Yeah, but for other reasons than messing with the casting, I thought, still interested in what had gone on at Juilliard to make a star student like Ana flunk out and run home.

I flipped to the next page and saw the actor bios. A black and white photo of Will stared back at me, sending a chill down my sweaty spine. I read over his paragraph.

Will Kemper (Mr. Darcy) has performed in many Pine Crest Productions throughout the years. He has played roles from Steinbeck to Shakespeare and everything in between, from backyard stages to Broadway. When he's not acting, he loves to hike around the beautiful Pacific Northwest with his wife, Bonnie.

I stopped. What? I read through it again, then I squinted up at Sarah. "I didn't know Will was on Broadway."

She beamed, nodding, but her happiness was quickly replaced with her previous nauseous pallor. "Earlier this year. He went to New York, said he was ready to make his dream happen. And he did."

Taking a few seconds to form my next sentence carefully, as to neither speak ill of the dead nor anger our current source of information, I licked my dry lips. "Uh, what brought him back here, then?"

Sarah sighed. "Well, he was in the chorus of a musical, so no big parts, but he thought it would help him get his foot in the door. The musical ran for three months and he was there faithfully every show, but when auditions opened for the next play, those jerks didn't cast him. He decided to come back to Pine Crest. That's when we met."

"Oh?" Alex asked.

I glanced over, knowing he was thinking the same thing I was.

"And how did Bonnie feel about him leaving, running

off to New York for months, having planned on staying for longer?" Alex jotted a few more things in his notebook.

Sarah shrugged. "It's the dream. Of course she supported it. I guess the plan was for her to join him if things went well. But he said they really grew apart, had been before he left, and their separation only made it worse." She shuffled "By the time he came back, he said they were done. I don't want you guys to think I'm some home-wrecker."

I shook my head, but Alex kept his face impassive. Gosh, he was so much better at that than me. No matter what I thought, my instinct was to ease her worries and tell her "of course we didn't think that, no one would," untrue as it was. And while I felt proud of myself for not saying those fake things, the absence of them definitely created an awkward air between us.

Alex moved on to questions about where Sarah had been on the morning of Will's murder and last night during the book-stabbing episode. She had witnesses for both of her alibis, and Alex jotted them down.

My eyes wandered to the books Bonnie had stacked on her director's desk. It looked like she was sticking pretty closely with the Austen theme. She had a copy of *Emma*, *Pride and Prejudice*, and even *Persua*—my throat went dry as my eyes traced the golden script of the title along the purple cloth-wrapped hardback. It was under a stack of papers, toward the top of one of the book piles, and sure, it was possible there was more than one copy like mine in Pine Crest, but…

I gulped, wild eyes flitting between the book and Alex. He was jotting down what Sarah was saying, but finally shot me a quick warning look. It started with a distinct "cut it out" quality, until he did a double take and caught the distress in my face. I tried making a few quick jerk motions with my head, toward the book on the desk, but Alex didn't seem to follow.

He shook his head and waited until it was clear Sarah was all done talking before saying, "Thank you for coming to me with this information. I'm so sorry, but would you excuse us for just a moment? I need to talk with Pepper about something, real quick." He sent her a bright, handsome smile, and she nodded, a bit entranced I think.

The three of us sat there for a moment in silence before Sarah's eyes widened and she said, "Oh. You want *me* to—got it." She pointed outside and jumped up, heading outside.

Alex turned toward me, his brown eyes an equal mix of annoyance and concern.

I pointed, mouth open to tell him about the book when his phone began ringing from his pocket. He sighed, pulling it out to read the screen.

"I need to take this. Sorry." He stood up and paced to the back of the tent as if it would afford him any kind of privacy.

But I was not on the phone—still didn't have a working one for that matter—and all I could do while I waited was stare down that book. I knew Alex would yell at me for touching it if it was evidence, but surely the papers sitting on top weren't of any consequence.

Using the desk as a temporary crutch, I pulled myself up and leaned forward so I could pick up the stack of scripts sitting on top of the copy of *Persuasion*. My heart hammered in my ears, pounding louder with each second as my eyes settled on the cover.

"Pepper, did you hear me?" Alex waved at me as he stepped closer, demanding my attention.

I shook my head. "Sorry, no."

Alex scratched his right eyebrow, which meant he must be confused. He shook his head. "That was Frank, down at the station."

"Yeah?" I said, willing him to spit it out.

His eyes locked onto mine. "Tommy just turned himself in for the murder of Will Kemper."

Shock felt like a punch to my gut, knocking the wind out of me. I gasped. Unable to speak, I shook my head, settling back into the chair.

Alex came over, sitting next to me, placing a concerned hand on my arm. "I'm... this is... I'm as shocked as you."

I felt like one of those creepy animatronic props on Disney rides, programmed to do the same thing over and over again. At that moment, the Shocked Pepper character was only set up to shake her head back-and-forth.

Breaking out of it, I said, "No. He couldn't have."

Alex sighed. "It appears he did." He rubbed a supportive hand up and down my arm.

Placing my hand over his to stop him, I caught his eyes with mine. "Then why does Bonnie have my book? And why does it have a slit where she shoved a knife through the front cover?" I asked, pointing to the book on Bonnie's desk.

A three-inch gash marred the purple cloth cover.

18

Alex bagged up the book as evidence, but then we raced out of the festival to get back to the station—well, raced isn't exactly what I would call what I was able to do on those crutches, but I clambered as quickly as I could.

It wasn't until Alex was driving down Main Street that I remembered Ana.

"Wait! I can't come with you to the station. I've got to go relieve Ana. What if she hasn't heard about Tommy yet?" I knew the answer even as I asked the question; the possibility of this news spreading slowly in Pine Crest was about as great as the infamous Mrs. Bennet keeping her mouth shut.

Alex nodded and pulled up next to the shop, not bothering to park. "You'll be okay?"

I nodded and planted a kiss on his rough cheek. I was gathering my temporary aluminum limbs, when he stopped me.

"Here, take this." He slipped something into my back jeans pocket.

I craned my neck to see his phone.

"Just in case, until we can get you a new one."

"Thanks." I smiled and hobbled out of the truck. It took me a second, fumbling with the door before I could get myself into the shop; the bell above me announcing my arrival—if all the racket I'd made hadn't already. I put on my best, concerned boss face and looked toward the register.

"Hey, honey." My mom waved from behind the customer she was helping.

"Mom?" I wobbled forward. "What are you doing here?"

She handed the customer their receipt, thanked them for coming, and then pulled me into a tight hug. "Look at you." She shook her head and clicked her tongue. "I heard about your accident last night and I came to check on you, but you weren't here. Just as I was about to leave, we got the news about Tommy, so I let Ana go to the station to see him." She shrugged. "If they even let her." Mom's face creased from worry. "Poor girl."

I nodded, swallowing the uncomfortable feeling sitting in my throat. "Especially since she and I so recently had a conversation about how Tommy could never have done something like this."

Mom tipped her head to one side. "I know. People can surprise you, that's for sure."

"Why would he kill Will, though?" I shook my head. "Over a part in a community production? That hardly seems worth it."

"Agreed, but it's possible you don't have all of the facts." Mom gave me a raised eyebrow—her don't be a know-it-all look.

I was too busy having an aha moment to catch her criticism. "True." I snapped my fingers. "The night before he was killed, Will was plotting how to get rid of Tommy. He mentioned digging up some dirt and using it to convince Tommy to bow out. What if Will found something?"

"Tommy's a famous actor now, he's bound to have some skeletons in his closet, or at least embarrassing cobwebs."

I tapped the pads of my fingers against my bottom lip as I thought. "I can't shake the feeling Bonnie is somehow involved in this. I mean, she had the book from last night in her tent."

Mom's face wrinkled in question and I realized that she may have heard about my accident from the townspeople, but probably didn't know the cause. I explained what had happened with the knife, book, and how I'd gotten so well-acquainted with the sidewalk.

Thinking aloud, I countered my own point. "But remember the note in Will's hand written on Duncan's stationary, and the video of Karla threatening Tommy? Those were both placed to throw us off the real killer's tracks."

"If that's the case, could Tommy have placed the book in Bonnie's tent to frame her, too?"

I shrugged. "And then turn himself in?" I shook my head. "That doesn't make sense." I didn't mention how betrayed I felt thinking of Tommy placing the warning in front of my shop after I'd defended him in front of Alex—or maybe it was less about betrayal and more about me seriously hating being wrong.

Returning to Jane Austen as a way to center myself in all of this, I thought about George Wickham. Was I being fooled by Tommy as Elizabeth had been by him? Darcy, ultimately, had been the one to set Lizzy straight about the man. *"Mr. Wickham is blessed with such happy manners as may ensure his making friends—whether he may be equally capable of retaining them, is less certain."*

Tommy, in all of his off-putting and narcissistic behavior, had managed to make me like him. But the man *was* an actor. What if it had all been a show to keep me from suspecting him?

After standing there in silent thought for a few seconds, Mom said, "You know who *would* know if there was anything out there someone could use to blackmail Tommy…"

Based on the girlish grin tugging at her mouth, I didn't even need to guess. "Duncan."

She nodded. "The police should be releasing him shortly. Here, I'll text him and see if he can stop by."

Chuckling, I said, "Oh, you two are texting now?"

"Just to set up our coffee date the other morning." She rolled her eyes in a way that would give most teens a run for their money. "He's been a little preoccupied since then."

I waved a hand. "Sure. Go for it. Can't hurt. In the meantime, I've got some stock to inventory. You gonna stick around?"

Mom nodded, her eyes already glued to her phone, fingers typing out a message to the man she'd been sure was innocent. Like I said, my mom is a great judge of character.

I GLANCED up from the stack of books I was hiding behind, trying to unsee the awkward reunion I'd just witnessed between my mom and Duncan.

Did she have to hug him?

I mean, come on. They'd only known each other for, like, a day. Suddenly, having dinner and half a coffee with a guy was grounds for hugging him when he was released from police custody. I rolled my eyes, first at her and then at myself. Gah. I knew I was acting like a brat about her interest in Duncan.

The two of them walked over to me, beaming happiness like some sort of too-bright floodlight, blinding you when you were perfectly happy walking in the dark.

"Pepper! Good to see you again." He flashed me his perfect movie-star smile. "Under much happier circumstances this time."

My lip curled slightly—of its own volition, I swear. "I would think seeing how a client of yours admitted to first-degree murder, it would probably warrant a different adjective than *happier*, but… your choice." I glared back at him.

Duncan cleared his throat. "Right. Very true."

Mom gave me a look that felt like something she reserved solely for people who lied on the witness stand. I focused on the book in front of me, but I could still feel the heat from her stare.

"So Duncan, the only thing we can think of in the way of a motive for Tommy to kill Will is that the man had managed to dig up some kind of dirt on your star. What do you think?" I asked.

Mom may have brought him here to flirt, but I wanted answers. Typing "Thomas King scandal" into the search engine, I looked over the results.

The manager's face tightened. "It's entirely possible. Between Thomas' PR agent and myself, we do our best to catch stories before they get to the bigger gossip sites, but every once in a while something slips through, or someone knows what they're looking for." He ran a hand over his chin—rough from a few days without a shave.

"What are they looking for?" I asked.

He nodded. "There's so much out there that's not even remotely true. You have to know what you're looking for or you'd be running around telling everyone Tommy's in an arranged marriage with Beyoncé and Jay-Z's firstborn."

Releasing a reluctant snort, I nodded. That happened to be the fourth thing that had shown up in my search. Okay, this guy knew his stuff. "Got it. What are we looking for then?" I moved a stack of books and swiveled the screen of my computer toward him.

"Yeah, none of this was new, or based in any reality. But there was something I'd been working to keep out of the press. I wasn't able to keep tabs on it while I was in custody, though, so let's see if it grew into anything new." Duncan ran his eyes over the screen for a moment before motioning for the keyboard, too. I slid it closer to him and he typed.

"Did I search for the wrong thing?"

"Not the wrong thing, just in the wrong place." More typing. "Thomas has a few very intense fan sites and they're usually the only ones who care about his family and super-personal stuff." He read the options that came up.

I craned my neck to see as my mother leaned closer. He was on a blog called *Our One True King*.

"Oh no. These people are insane."

Duncan raised his eyebrows and clicked on one of the blog links titled, *Ana King*. There are far fewer posts about Ana than all things Tommy, but there were a handful, all titled things like, *Dropping Out?*, *Running Home*, and *What Will She Do Now?*

Shaking his head, Duncan pushed the computer back toward me. "None of these are new, either." He sighed. "Oh well, I suppose anything having to do with Ana is less of a worry now her brother's in custody for murder."

My shoulders slumped in defeat.

His hand landed on mine. "The internet, believe it or not, is not the be-all-end-all when it comes to blackmail. I have a few sources I'll get in touch with and let you know if I hear of anything Will could've gotten his hands on, something that would've pushed Thomas over the edge." Duncan patted my hand before removing his.

Mom nodded. "Will was an actor. He may have known someone in Hollywood who had information Tommy didn't want getting out." She smiled at Duncan.

"Great. Thanks." My insides flipped uncomfortably as I watched her look at this new man.

I wanted to be happy for her, but I couldn't help how seeing her with Duncan made me miss my dad something fierce and full-bodied. It was as if I could picture him standing there next to me. His scruffy, red beard would be slightly too long to be able to be called "well-kept." That mop of auburn hair ruffled from the way he constantly ran his hands through it while he read—just as Alex was known to do to his. He wore ink stains on his fingers like Mom wore her trusty black-patent heels.

But watching my perfectly poised mother with the harrowingly handsome Duncan seemed too… matchy-matchy, to be honest. Relationships were built on opposites, right? Liv in all her serious, businesslady-ness fitting perfectly with Carson, who always had a joke ready to keep the situation light. Alex and his tendency to be too serious, too organized, was just the match for never-predictable, unorganized me.

Or was I simply mad that my mom was showing interest in someone other than my dad?

I bit my lip as I watched Duncan. He and Mom had moved from Tommy to his time spent at the station. "I thought they were joking when they told me I was free to go." He chuckled, moving closer to Mom.

The relief he talked about was written so clearly in his

features. His bright eyes, the way his lips couldn't be tempted into anything other than a smile. But there was something else there as well.

"Well, I should probably go get myself cleaned up. I hope the inn held my room and my belongings while I was occupied." He winked in my direction. "I'll let you know if I hear anything, Pepper." Then he faced Mom, holding his arm out. "Care to keep me company on the walk?" he asked.

Mom's cheeks went pink and she nodded. "You got it covered here now?" she asked, looking over at me.

Without hesitation—or attitude, this time—I said, "I got it. You two go have fun."

My mother's eyes sparkled in a firm thank you, and then she and Duncan left with a tinkle of the bell over the front door.

The stacks of books I'd piled on the counter suddenly seemed dauntingly tall. But I had a business to run and so I powered through, pausing from time to time to wait on customers. By the time I closed up, I was starting to see a figurative light at the end of the tunnel, just as the literal sunlight outside was disappearing behind the mountains. I was beat, though, and my foot was killing me after being on it all day. Inventory would have to wait until tomorrow.

I locked the shop door and then went to shut down the computer. The results from Duncan's search about Ana were still listed on the screen. Fingers twiddling over the mouse for a second, my curiosity got the better of me and I clicked through a few of the sites. It wasn't anything I hadn't already learned from Karla, but I tried to see it through the new lens of Tommy's confession. Would he have been so worried about protecting Ana's secret that he would've killed Will to do so?

I kicked the toe of my shoe into the register counter out of frustration. Failing one quarter of college didn't seem *so* bad, honestly. I'd known a lot of classmates who were taking classes through the fall to complete their degrees, having one quarter where they'd imbibed a little too much in their newfound freedom or had chosen a major only to realize it really wasn't for them. Clicking on another link, I skimmed the story to see if there was anything more I was missing.

Keeping Duncan's advice in mind, I found it pretty safe to say the article's claim Ana had gotten pregnant by the writer and star of the Broadway hit *Hamilton*, Lin Manuel Miranda, was garbage. The next article's suggestion that drugs were involved wasn't as farfetched, but having been around Ana, I felt it was pretty safe to say the girl was clean as a whistle. And, again, a drug problem didn't seem worthy of homicide in my book.

Each of the links had gotten their hands on pictures of Ana, some of her on her own and a few of her joining Tommy on the red carpet for a special occasion.

But it was the picture contained in the fifth article I clicked on that made me gasp.

Black and white, but still clear as day, was a series of photographs of Ana with a man. Holding hands, walking down the street, laughing, kissing. And in each picture, the man was the same.

Will.

19

The pictures of Ana and Will blurred as my brain tried to focus on too many things at once. Clues, pictures, questions. But mostly, motive. The one thing that had been missing in Tommy's sudden confession.

Until now.

I thought back to watching Tommy and Will interact, the way they'd looked like rabid dogs about to lunge at the other's throat. Tommy had to have known about Will and Ana. He'd simply covered his tracks by letting Karla believe he didn't. And then planted evidence that implicated Duncan, Karla, Bonnie, anyone but himself. Threatening me when I started to get close.

I sighed and shook my head.

No. It still didn't make sense. Why would he threaten me if he was only going to turn himself in the next day? Why would he go through all of the effort to plant incriminating evidence on everyone with a motive?

My mind flashed back to my encounter at the fair with Will, Tommy, and Ana. Had Ana stepped behind her brother to hide or had Tommy stepped in front of his sister?

Glancing back at the pictures of Ana and Will, it clicked into place.

He wasn't *giving* up, he was *covering* up.

Tommy had turned himself in to protect Ana, the real killer!

Ana in New York, at Juilliard. Will cast in his small part on Broadway, there for a handful of months. Had Will looked her up when he'd gotten into the city? Or maybe they simply bumped into each other and grabbed a drink, two people from the same small hometown. It could've easily turned into something much more. And then he'd left, leaving Ana depressed and disillusioned, dropping out a few weeks later to come after him. It all made sense.

Alex needed to know this. Grabbing my purse, I went to dig out my phone. Just as I remembered it was at home, broken, I heard the back door open and shut. I froze. I'd only given a few people the key to the shop. My heart hammered in my chest, hoping to see my mom or Maggie.

Ana entered, her eyes red and puffy, her hands clutching a small book as if it were her only lifeline.

"Hey." I could feel my voice shaking—or was that my whole body? Dropping my purse, I took a deep breath. "I'm... so sorry I wasn't here." I grabbed one of my crutches and hobbled forward, hoping it looked like I was moving to comfort her and not like I was trying to get closer to the front door.

She waved a hand. "It's okay. I—I—" A few sobs broke through before she could hold the rest back. "I thought I would come help you with inventory, to keep my mind off things."

I glanced back at the computer. The screen was facing away from us, but still held the picture of Ana and Will. If she walked over there, she would know. I needed to get out of here.

"Oh, I was about to head home…" Looking at my foot, I pointed down. "Ice my foot, get it elevated."

Ana nodded and walked closer, her fingers still wrapped around the book. "Right." She shook her head. "I forgot. Sorry."

It was then I caught sight of the pink flower on the binding. Panic moved through me in hot waves.

That wasn't a book. It was my diary from high school. Why did she have it?

"Oh, haha, that's *not* part of the inventory." I reached forward, clambering toward Ana with my one crutch, eyeing the front door as I did so. I'd stupidly locked the shop already and it would take me at least three tries to get the door open, if I even made it over there before she could get to me.

Instead of handing it over, Ana clutched the book tighter.

"Ana, seriously, it's mine." I dropped my voice into an I'm-your-boss register. "It's private," I added.

Her puffy eyes watched me. "I know." She sniffed.

Worry gripped my lungs and I stifled a gasp. She knew more than just about the diary. There was something about the tightness in her tone. I leaned on my crutch in an effort to steady myself.

"Then what are you doing with it?" I asked, not quite sure why I was continuing the charade.

She tipped her head to one side, but didn't answer me. Instead, sniffing and wiping her nose with a tissue in her free hand.

"Ana, I know it was you." My body flashed hot and cold as I breathed out the words.

Ana simply stepped one foot closer to me. She may have been able to scare off the other people who'd gotten in her way, but I wasn't going down so easily. I shuffled forward, standing up as straight as I could in my battered body. Ana didn't budge, her breath slow and calm.

"You were mad at Will for leaving, for running back to Bonnie when he didn't get another part in New York. You wanted to get revenge."

Ana shrugged, but I could see the emotion behind her eyes. The sweet sparkle when she smiled was lost, replaced with fire, hatred. Still she remained silent. It was then that it truly hit me; I was in a locked store with a murderer. I couldn't see anything on her other than my diary, but who knew if she had another knife up her sleeve.

Finally and suddenly, the absolute need to escape grasped at my lungs, but I'd made my way into the direct middle of the shop, Ana blocking the front door. Of course that's what she'd been doing. I could never make it to the back door with this crutch and a bum ankle before she caught me.

It was getting dark outside, but maybe I could try to scream for help, maybe there was someone out there. My eyes moved to the front windows. In the dusky light, I could see Ana's car parked in one of the diagonal spots in front of the shop. I almost looked away, but the car next to hers caught my attention. It was the same one Alex and I had seen on our hike to the lake on his mom's birthday.

The floorboard behind me creaked. Before I could turn around, something hard collided with the back of my head and everything disappeared.

Literally Gone

MY HEAD FELT like it had been split in half. I winced, and felt tape pull at my face with the movement. It covered my mouth and the rubbery scent of it was cloying in its intensity. I blinked, but was met with inky darkness whether my eyes were open or closed. The air was stale and suffocatingly hot as I tried to pull it steadily in through my nose, surrounding me like a wool blanket I hadn't asked for.

Something was cinched tight around my ankles and wrists. The sprained ankle screamed out at me and I could tell I was lying on my bruised hip from the pain that radiated from that spot as I squirmed. Trying to relieve what pain I could, I attempted to roll back and move on to my other side. My head thunked into something solid, sending a whole new round of pain spiking through my skull. Unable to move sideways, I tried to straighten my legs, but found my container small and confining that direction as well.

I froze as I heard voices outside. I couldn't make out exactly what they were saying, but Ana's sweet tone was easily recognizable. The thought of how I'd trusted her—how everyone had—made me sick.

What made me more sick, however, was the voice that answered Ana's. From its hissing tone and slight British accent, there could be no question who it belonged to. Nate Newton. Tears formed in my eyes, ones I couldn't possibly wipe away tied up like this. Disbelief washed through me in waves of nausea. Nate was involved in this? He'd been the one to knock me in the back of the head?

My thoughts flashed back to my impromptu setup attempt with Ana and Nate the other day. Ana had dismissed the idea so quickly. Now I realized she must've been covering up their real relationship. Maybe they were *already* in a romantic entanglement and had conspired to kill her ex together.

Just then two car doors slammed shut and an engine rumbled to life. My nostrils flared as my heart rate sped up. I couldn't pull in enough air. I couldn't move. I couldn't scream for help. My body rocked back into the solid object behind me as I felt the car pull forward, pull away.

Taking me away.

I tried to scream, but I couldn't even hear myself over the engine. There was no hope anyone else might hear my muffled cries.

For the first few minutes, I tried wiggling my fingers and moving my wrists to see if I could work my way out of my bonds. They were tied tight and I didn't succeed in loosening a bit of rope. In the movement, however, my tied hands rubbed up against the back pocket of my jeans.

Hope hit me like a disaster movie tsunami wave. Alex's phone! In all of my grogginess from being hit in the back of the head, I'd completely forgotten that he'd given it to me. I couldn't call Alex, his phone here with me, but I was sure he had Frank's number in his contacts.

With a renewed sense of adrenaline, I maneuvered my arms so I could awkwardly slip the phone from the back pocket with my bound hands. After clutching it for a happy second, I positioned it so my right thumb was on the home button. I pressed down and the trunk lit up with the light from the screen. I held the phone up and twisted my body until I could see the screen.

The still-locked screen.

This wasn't my phone, so it wouldn't unlock at the touch of my finger. A puff of disappointment left me in the form of a quick exhale.

I took a fortifying breath. That was okay. I knew Alex's code. Craning my neck, I looked back at the screen, straining with my thumb to try to reach the three. Hands backward and bound, it seemed almost impossible. But I shifted the phone down slightly with my other fingers and my thumb landed on the three. The celebration in my mind was cut short when the car seemed to move from pavement to a rockier, rougher road. The sedan shuddered and bounced on the new terrain. A large pothole sent me and the object behind me airborne for a second or two.

My panicked fingers tried to hold on to the phone, but as I landed it slipped from my grasp. I heard the phone bounce and settle somewhere at the back of the trunk, way out of my reach. Still, I tried, searching the felt lining of the trunk in the small area behind me I could reach. Tears filled my eyes and I tried to breathe through the dread as my fingers came up empty.

After that, an odd sort of calm settled over me as the car drove farther and farther away. There was nothing I could do until they took me out of this trunk. Which meant my only hope was to appeal to Nate. We'd been friends—of sorts—over the past year. Maybe if I could separate him from Ana, look him in those almost-black eyes, and… well, beg, plead, hope for mercy.

For a while, I tried to pay attention to how many right and left turns we were making, how long did we drive on each road. I'd seen a character do something similar in a movie once. She figured out how to get home by working backward from what she remembered. The problem was, I wasn't very good with maps in the best of circumstances. Plus, the girl in that movie had been kidnapped, kept in a remote location for weeks. There was not a doubt in my mind Ana was taking me somewhere to get rid of me. She meant to kill me, not keep me. And she had help.

When the car began to climb, rocking me forward slightly, I knew where I was—well, where we were headed.

There was only one trail I knew of that steep, that riddled with potholes.

The trail up to the lake.

It made sense, I suppose. It was where Alex and I had seen her car during our hike over the weekend. That must've been Nate's car parked next to hers. My forehead wrinkled. Nate didn't have a car, though. At least, I didn't think he did. He borrowed his grandma's car occasionally, but it was an old yellow Volvo, not the red sporty thing I'd seen alongside Ana's black sedan, the same one she'd had since high school.

I rolled my eyes at myself in the darkness of the trunk. *You didn't know Nate was in cahoots with Ana in a murder, though, so maybe you also didn't realize he'd gotten a car.*

True. Nate hadn't even been on my suspect radar. Embarrassing as it was to admit, Ana hadn't really either. I'd been so focused on Duncan and then Karla and then Bonnie I hadn't noticed anyone else. Ana's planted evidence had done its job, distracting me and the police from the real kill—

The car skidded to a halt. All sense of calm immediately dissipated as both car doors opened. I jumped as they slammed shut. Eyes wide, I waited for the trunk to open.

I heard Ana say, "Let's get this over with, quick."

"The quicker the better," a female voice replied.

Wait. There were three of them? I strained to listen for Nate's deep hiss, but heard nothing.

Whereas I'd felt collected—dare I say ready?—before, this woman's voice in place of Nate's scattered any whisper of a plan I'd managed to piece together on the drive up to the lake. So when the trunk thunked open, I screamed and squirmed instead of trying to locate Nate as planned.

Ana's face was like porcelain against the night's sky. I

could make out the ghostly ridges of my beloved Cascade Mountains behind her, but nothing more. She leaned forward, grabbing a hold of my shoulders. I felt someone do the same with my legs, but Ana's body blocked my view of them.

Then there was the pain. It shot through my entire foot and leg as they picked me up, wrenching my hurt ankle as if on purpose, as if to hobble me even more. Evil, but smart. The forest, the craggy mountain ridges, the inky blackness of the lake, it all swirled around me as they carried me away from the car and then flung me down on the sloping granite lakeshore.

I landed on my already bruised hip. A cry ripped out of me, only to be blocked by the suffocating strip of tape covering my mouth. Shoes crunched on the rock and gravel as their footsteps returned to the car. I heard a grunt as they seemed to lug something else out from the trunk. The solid thing behind me.

Wheeling my head and feet, I managed to turn over, facing the direction of the car, away from the pitch-black water of the lake. When I did, my eyes went wide and my nostrils flared as my heartbeat quickened.

Ana's fingers gripped the head of a three-foot marble sculpture of Jane Austen. Bonnie held the base as they carried it over to me.

Her eyes met mine, a grin spreading across her face.

20

"Can we take the tape off her mouth, please?" Bonnie said between grunts as they set the marble bust down next to me. She swiped her curly hair off her forehead. "The look on her face is too good. I want to hear how surprised she is."

Ana went back to the trunk, pulling out more rope. "I don't care. We're miles away from anyone. No one would hear her if she screamed." Ana paused, reaching into the trunk. "Or called." She pulled out Alex's phone and hopelessness settled over me. After a quick second, she chucked it into the lake.

Bonnie laughed and took a step toward me, leaning down in my face. "Nah. On second thought, it's more fun that she'll die never knowing."

Having just watched Ana sink my only remaining lifeline, I shrugged. I could see it all too easily now I knew they were working together, but none of that mattered. I was still going to die.

"Oh, you think you've figured it out?" Bonnie asked,

having interpreted my gesture as sarcastic rather than discouraged. She leaned down and ripped off the tape.

I couldn't see much in the dark, but I was pretty sure most of my lip skin was still attached to the tape. I pressed what was left of them together for a quick second, then ran my tongue over the stinging surface. The skin around my lips pulsed with pain.

"Come on, detective Pepper, tell us how we did it." Bonnie crossed her arms and waited.

Anger rose up in me. I strained against the ropes holding my wrists together and for the first time, felt them loosen. I wasn't sure what I would do even if I got my hands free, but I had to try, which meant I needed to stall whatever was going to happen with me and Jane Austen.

And I knew just how to do it.

Pulling in a deep breath, I began to tell her what I knew. "Will went to New York to try to make his dream of acting on Broadway a reality." My voice was hoarse from screaming into the tape. I worked my hands to create space within the bonds as I talked. "Juilliard and Broadway must be near each other in the city. Ana and Will ran into each other at a party or a restaurant, I'm guessing."

Ana tipped her head to one side as she worked at untangling the rope she'd pulled from the trunk.

"They started an affair that consumed all of their time, making Ana flunk a few classes that semester and causing Will's performance as a member of the chorus in his musical to be sub par. So when the short run of his show was over and he auditioned for the next, he didn't get a callback." I used my fingertips to nudge and push the rope. "Frustrated, he ran back here to Pine Crest. Ana, already in hot water with most of her classes, became depressed and angry, letting it simmer for a few weeks after he'd left."

At this, Ana's jaw clenched tight. She focused on the rope.

"He told you he was going to leave Bonnie. Didn't he?" I tried to meet her eyes, but she wouldn't look at me. "Only to go right back to her." I turned my attention to Bonnie.

"Bonnie, you didn't expect Will to come back so soon, but you must've been relieved. You didn't really want to move to New York. Plus, you'd gotten the director position for the festival."

I could now move my wrists apart until there was a good half inch of space between them. I kept working.

"You also thought maybe the experience had humbled your husband. If he'd been brought down a peg or two, maybe he'd stop sleeping around and be faithful to just you."

Bonnie's eyes narrowed, and she shifted her feet.

"Ana can't have been the first one." Even in the dark, I could see a redness rise from Bonnie's neck and into her face. I knew I was getting somewhere. "But he didn't stop, did he?" I remembered Sarah's confession. "He started up something with your own assistant. Right behind your back."

At the mention of Sarah, both of the women stiffened. Their apparent anger made me quite sure if I didn't get out of this, there would be another body in their wake. Sarah was in danger, too.

"I'm not sure how the two of you met. Probably through the festival since you were playing piano for some of the plays, Ana. One of you must've caught him with Sarah. I'm guessing you, Bonnie. Because Ana had to maintain an air of innocence, enough to lure him into her brother's trailer that morning."

Rope finally ready, Ana knelt next to the Jane bust and

let out a light laugh as she tied one end around her marble neck. I swallowed uncomfortably. I could almost slip one of my wrists free.

"And since Bonnie became a suspect once your planted evidence framing Duncan and Karla was thrown aside, you planted the book on Bonnie to make us think she'd simply been another victim of false evidence. But you didn't count on Tommy turning himself in."

Ana tightened the rope around Jane with one last pull.

"Which is why you needed to plant the diary on me, to get him out. I'm guessing there's also a confession note alongside it sitting in my shop right now."

Bonnie huffed. "On the computer."

I paid no attention to her, focusing on Ana. "How'd your brother figure it out?"

Ana's lip curled. "I told you they asked a lot of questions during those dinners."

Ah, the dinner with Tommy and her uncle the night before. I could almost get one of my hands free. I needed to keep this going a little bit longer.

"So it never was Tommy's life in danger." I nodded. "You needed to paint him as the victim, so the police wouldn't look to him as a suspect. You know, if you weren't going to spend the rest of your life in prison, Ana, I'd say you could have a real future as an actor."

Ana smiled then stood, the other end of the rope in her hand. Seeing her coming toward me made me panic and I tried using one quick motion to pull my wrist free. It slipped out, but the movement was too noticeable. Ana's smile faded.

"Retie that." She snapped at Bonnie. "Tighter this time."

Any hope of escape drained out of me as Bonnie scurried behind me. She grabbed my free hand and wrapped the rope around it, cinching it so tight I cried out.

No longer trying to stall, I simply wanted to know the last part of the story, so I asked, "How'd you get Will to the trailer, Ana?"

She stepped behind me to check my hands were secure. I craned my neck to see her.

But it was Bonnie who answered. "Psh. No man can resist a note asking for 'one last time together.' Especially when costumes are involved."

"You lured him in, Ana, and then you stabbed him, Bonnie, with the knife in Duncan's box of fishing supplies." My gaze flicked between the two of them, standing behind me, leering over me.

They looked at each other. Ana shrugged. "Will ruined both our lives because he disappeared. When we needed him the most, he was gone. We just made it permanent. And now we're making sure you're *literally* gone, too." She bent down and tied the other end of the shorter rope around my legs while Bonnie kicked over the bust and rolled it closer to the water.

Now that my eyes had fully adjusted, I saw we were not on a sloping section of the lakeshore, but a small ledge, an overhang I recognized. We used to jump off of it in high school because it dropped us into the deepest part of the lake and had a low, sloping section next to it we could use to climb out. Ana rolled me closer to the edge.

My hands strained against the ropes, thoughts frantic as I watched Bonnie standing at the very edge of the drop, foot on top of the marble statue, holding it in place.

"So long," Ana said, and I watched, wide-eyed. Bonnie kicked the Jane Austen bust over the edge. The rope between us snapped tight and the momentum of the probably two-hundred-pound statue yanked me, feet first over the edge. Air rushed around me. I closed my eyes.

I heard the stone figure splash into the lake moments before I plunged into the cold water. It engulfed me in an icy straightjacket, holding too tight to every bit of my body. Twisting and wrenching my wrists, I tried to break free as I sank.

And sank. Twenty feet at least, if memory served me from high school.

The *clunk* of the marble settling onto the lake floor echoed around me. I opened my eyes, but it was blurry and mostly dark. Air burned in my lungs, sitting there too long. I let it out a little at a time, envious of the bubbles escaping up to the surface.

Floating there on the end of the short rope that chained me to Jane Austen, I began searching my surroundings for something, anything. There was a large rock jutting out of the lake bottom next to me. Turning around, I maneuvered myself until my wrists and the ropes holding them tight rubbed against one of the sharp edges. I moved my arms up and down as I tried to saw through my binds.

Flinching, each time I would accidentally get skin instead of rope, I kept it up for a few seconds, letting a little breath go in a cloud of bubbles. But then my lungs really began to burn and my head felt light.

I think I would've closed my eyes, pulled in a breath-full of water if something hadn't entered the water above me at just that moment. As it was, my eyes widened, watching the figure and the beam of light it brought with it. The swimmer shined the light right at me, blinding me for all intents and purposes.

Panic coursed through me. Had Ana or Bonnie come after me to finish the job? Was I taking too long to drown? I thrashed, crying out as I accidentally banged my hands into the sharp rock behind me.

I tried to look again. The person was approaching, flashlight now pointed down at my feet, so it no longer blinded me. But the relief was short-lived when I saw the knife glinting in their hand. I pulled in a deep gasp, but was met with water instead of air.

My eyes fluttered shut.

I SPUTTERED AND COUGHED, throwing up water, heaving as it wretched out of me. A hand slapped me on the back as I sat up, propping myself up with one arm. Lake water puddled around me.

Blinking the last beads of water from my eyes, I looked up. Millions of bright stars twinkled back at me. I smiled.

"Hello to you too," I said in a raspy voice, then broke into a fit of coughs.

Arms wrapped around me, tight, and I turned my attention to the equally sopping wet body crouched next to me. The scent of peppermint and soap made my heart skip. Alex. Hands cupped my cheeks and then his face appeared in front of me. It was creased into a happy smile, as if he'd been greeted by the stars as well.

Water dripped from his hair, onto his nose, trailing down his chin. "Mi pimienta, I'm so glad you're okay." His hands let go of my face and then patted down my arms as if just to make sure I was in one piece.

Everything still felt like it was spinning, and I couldn't be sure if I was going to cough or throw up again. But I nodded. I was alive.

My gaze traveled down to my feet and the pieces of rope

lying haphazardly in piles there. Suddenly, my heart stopped. My head whipped around to where Ana's car had been parked.

It was gone.

Turning my frantic attention back to Alex, I asked, "Where—?" anything more was cut off by more coughing.

His eyebrows furrowed together. "I got here right as Bonnie dropped that statue into the water. I couldn't cuff them *and* save you, so I had to let them go." He looked away, as if unable to meet my eyes.

Picking my hands up off the ground, I brought them up, cupping his face and pointing it back toward me. My body wobbled a little without the extra support of my arms, but Alex's brown eyes steadied me.

"You saved my life." I leaned forward and kissed him, hoping he didn't mind I'd just thrown up a bunch of lake water.

He didn't. After a few seconds, he pulled away from the kiss, eyes piercing into mine. Alex's lips parted, but before he could say anything his radio squawked from his belt.

"Valdez, you there? Did you find Pepper?" Frank's voice came through the static.

He reached down to grab it, pressing down the button. "Got her. We're going to need some medical assistance, though."

"Aid car's already on its way up. Might take a second. That road's pretty tight."

"Thanks, Frank." He left his finger off the button for a second, eyes meeting mine. Then he pressed down again. "Any luck apprehending the suspects?"

We stared at the radio. It crackled for what seemed like forever.

"Roger that. Had a nice greeting party for them waiting down here at the bottom of the trail."

My shoulders slumped forward and I leaned into Alex, relief filling my whole body.

"Here, stay close to me. I don't want you to get too cold," Alex said as he helped me to my feet—well, foot.

The lights from the ambulance bounced up the trail. My fingers gripped the still-soaking white T-shirt he wore. It clung to him in all of the right places, reminding me of the iconic Darcy swimming scene from the BBC *Pride and Prejudice* miniseries.

Grinning, I plucked at the fabric on his bicep. It made a *thwick* sound as it suctioned back to his arm.

He shot me an amused grin. "What?"

"Nothing." I looked down for a second, hiding my own smile. "Just… where's the rest of your uniform?"

"It got hot on my run up here." Alex smiled.

"Well, between you and Mr. Darcy, I think you might win a wet-shirt contest."

"You know," he said, rolling his eyes. "That *wasn't* in the novel. They added the scene to the screenplay. As an Austen fan, I would expect you to know that."

I shrugged. "Of course I know it wasn't in the book. But do you really think there's a woman alive who cares?"

Alex chuckled. "Point taken."

We watched the ambulance amble over the last bit of the trail and then turn toward where we stood at the edge of the lake.

Just then, something struck me. I looked over at him. "How *did* you find me?"

"Nate."

"What?" I remembered hearing his voice in the trunk.

"I passed him when I was heading into the bookshop.

He said he'd just seen Ana leaving with Bonnie, so he didn't think you were there."

Sighing out of relief, I said, "So Nate wasn't part of any of this. He simply happened to be walking by right after they'd shoved me in the trunk."

Alex nodded. "When I went inside the shop, I saw the note 'you' left." He cleared his throat.

And the diary entry. Oh no. If there was any heat left in my body, I would've blushed. As it was, I just wanted to change the subject. "I still don't get it. How'd you know they took me here?"

Alex smiled. "My phone. In your back pocket." He pointed.

Grimacing, I looked over at the lake and then shook my head. "Not still in my pocket. Ana found it and chucked it in the lake. I'm sorry, but I think it's a goner."

Alex shrugged. "I can get a new phone. What I can't get is a new Pepper." He leaned down to kiss me again.

The sharp slamming of doors brought me back to where we were. I pulled away to see the ambulance parked next to us and the paramedics rushing toward me.

"We'll take her from here, Alex," Fiona, one of the local EMTs, said. "What'd you get yourself into this time?" she asked as she helped me to the truck.

21

The actors took one last bow then broke off as the audience stood and surged forward. A particularly large group formed around Tommy as he shot each fan a smarmy smile and swiped a hand through his hair. Alex pulled me tight, planting a kiss on the top of my head, careful to avoid the back where I now sported a lovely gash, compliments of Bonnie.

"Tommy's pretty good," Carson said, turning around from where he and Liv sat on the picnic blanket in front of us. "Still can't believe he decided to go through with this when his sister was arrested just two days ago."

"The show must go on," Liv said, quoting Tommy from his interview that morning.

"Not for Duncan from the sounds of it," I said.

"Whoa, is his career really finished now that Tommy fired him?" Carson asked.

I shook my head. "Not because of Tommy, but by choice. Apparently life in Hollywood has been completely stressing him out the last few years." I thought back to how remorseful Duncan had seemed when he'd told us how he'd snapped at Tommy and Karla upon arriving in Pine Crest.

"Can't blame the guy," Alex mumbled, eyeing Tommy.

"Mom said he's leaving Hollywood and wants to come live here," I added, the idea seeming less and less terrible the more I thought about it.

Liv smiled. "That's awesome. I'm so happy for your mom, Peps. I'm sure his life will be a lot less stressful without having to deal with Tommy and other actors like him." She tipped her head as she looked back toward the green stage. "But I do have to agree with Carson. Annoying as the guy is, Tommy actually made a pretty believable Darcy."

"Told you so." I shrugged.

"Uh oh." Alex cocked an eyebrow at me. "This something I should be worried about?" He bumped into me to show me he was joking.

"He is tolerable; but not handsome enough to tempt me," I said, quoting Mr. Darcy.

Pulling me tighter, he said, "Good answer."

"You're the only tall, broodingly handsome man I want." I sent him a wink.

The sun was setting, throwing pinks and oranges across the sky like a toddler painting for the very first time. Alex's smile gave the sunset stiff competition. The summer air breezed past us, gently feathering my hair and the bandage hidden at the back of my skull. Alex repositioned the pillows he'd brought to keep my ankle elevated.

Luckily, Bonnie and Ana hadn't succeeded in breaking any of my bones two nights ago, but the doctor had said I would need to stay off my ankle as much as possible for a week. Alex was taking it upon himself to make sure I followed her directions.

There had been a different something in his eyes after

he'd pulled me out of the water that night. In the moment, I'd assumed it was fear and adrenaline, a mixture created by the icy water and murderers. But it was still there the next morning when he'd come over to check on me. And again today when he'd come to pick me up for the closing show of AustenFest, *Pride and Prejudice*.

It wasn't a tightness, exactly, but a quality that hadn't been in those lovely brown eyes before. That, added to the way he looked at me every five seconds, and I was starting to think there was something wrong.

My stomach clenched uneasily, reminding me that he'd probably read the entry in my fifteen-year-old diary about Tommy. He said he'd stopped by the shop before figuring out I was in trouble the other night. Ana had left it behind, setting me up as a way to get Tommy off the hook. Embarrassment rose in hot waves in my neck.

"Alex," I looked away from the celebrating thespians and their families, facing him. "I—"

I couldn't get anything more out because his lips were covering mine. Had we been in an Austen novel, this kiss would have signaled the happy ending.

As if reading my thoughts, when he was done he leaned forward, whispering in my ear, "I cannot fix on the hour, or the look, or the words, which laid the foundation, but I love you, Pepper Brooks."

The most wonderful tickle danced down my spine. Sure, the man had quoted Darcy, but all I cared about was the last part of his statement.

"I love you, too," I whispered back.

Liv cleared her throat. Alex and I looked over at my best friend, a huge grin stretched across her face.

"We'll—er—give you two a little space," Carson said, grabbing Liv's hand. "Let's go talk to the man of the hour." He and Liv headed over toward the crowd around Tommy.

Alex leaned his forehead against mine, then closed his eyes. "I can't believe he's coming out of this looking like the hero."

Sighing, I said, "Well, can you honestly say you expected anything different from the famous Thomas King?"

After apprehending Bonnie and Ana, the police had released a mostly devastated Tommy. He'd come by my apartment the next day to apologize for putting my life in danger.

"I honestly never thought she'd go after you," he'd said.

"People do desperate things when they're mentally unwell," Alex had countered, standing next to me and crossing his arms, a clear sign it was time for Tommy to go.

And Tommy had, but Alex's statement must've stuck with the man, because within the hour the news stories began to change. Thomas King's little sister being arrested for conspiracy to murder and attempted murder was a juicy story, one every news site had latched onto. But when Thomas King sent in a video—clearly shot by Karla in his trailer that afternoon—apologizing to his sister for not noticing her signs of clinical depression and mental unrest, the news sites began playing it on what seemed like a continuous loop.

In the video, Tommy pledged a quarter of his wages for five years, to go toward depression awareness campaigns and treatment. That, in addition to how he'd tried to sacrifice himself in his sister's place, and Thomas King emerged from the whole thing a hero.

"That's okay," I said, threading my fingers through Alex's. "I know who the real hero is."

He wrapped an arm around me and we watched Liv

and Carson congratulating Tommy, who sent a smile and a wave toward the two of us. We waved back, but I doubt Alex smiled.

"I guess Jane Austen was right," Alex said after a few seconds.

I looked over at him.

"You cannot trust first impressions. It takes much more to get to know someone's true character."

Nodding, I thought of the charming Wickham, fooling everyone only to show his slimy ways at the bitter end. *Much like Ana and Bonnie*, I thought. *Will, too*. Not that he deserved to die, but he'd been far from the lovable actor he seemed on the surface. Tommy had surprised me as well. His publicity stunt aside, the man was kinder and had much more integrity than I'd once assumed. Heck, I'd even made the same incorrect snap judgment with Alex when we'd first met last year. I spent the first few weeks thinking he was awful and stuck up before getting to know the kind, sweet person behind his serious surface. A lot like Elizabeth and Mr. Darcy, I mused, smiling to myself.

"True," I said at last. "And speaking of someone we greatly misjudged, you and I are going to be late for drinks with Mom and Duncan if we don't hurry." I glanced down at my watch.

Alex stood, then helped me up next. "You don't think it's going to be a little awkward that I arrested the guy and now your mom is dating him?"

I laughed. "Oh no. It's going to be *incredibly* awkward." Patting his chest lightly, I added, "But we've survived worse."

Shaking his head, Alex chuckled and started packing up the pillows and folding the blanket we'd been sitting on. We waved goodbye to Liv and Carson then headed toward the bookstore to drop off our stuff. Mountains towered above the small town as we walked off the park grass and onto the sidewalk that would lead us into Pine Crest.

I breathed in deeply, contentedly.

"So tell me more about this diary you kept when you were younger," Alex said.

"Um…" I felt my face heat up. "Bet I can beat you to the bookstore," I said, picking up the pace on my crutches, leaving Alex behind.

His laughter followed me down the street.

Don't miss the next installment of Pepper Brooks Cozy Mysteries, *Literally Offed*.

Thoreau found peace in the woods. All Pepper finds is trouble.

Nothing ruins a camping trip faster than a dead body. Pepper Brooks planned a peaceful week in the woods with friends to get away from the stress of daily life. When her dog, Hamburger, sniffs out a murder victim, suddenly the woods feel as far from the tranquil Walden Pond as possible.

Pepper and Alex refuse to let law enforcement brush the case aside… they know there's more to the story. Their investigation unearths long-buried secrets from Pine Crest's past, some of which hit uncomfortably close to home.

This case is more than a murder mystery. For Pepper, it just got personal.

Read book four now!

ALSO BY ERYN SCOTT

The Pepper Brooks Cozy Mystery Series
Pebble Cove Teahouse Mysteries
The Stoneybrook Mysteries
Whiskers and Words Mysteries

ABOUT THE AUTHOR

Eryn Scott lives in the Pacific Northwest with her husband and their quirky animals. She loves classic literature, musicals, knitting, and hiking. She writes cozy mysteries.

Join her mailing list to learn about new releases and sales!

www.erynscott.com

540-776-6500
Hampton Inn
$165.44

Made in the USA
Middletown, DE
29 February 2024